Blessing Abiaka's other interesting book.

I0571082

1

Grandpa Story

Grandpa Christopher is a big time storyteller and songwriter. During the summertime, he writes his own stories and reads them to his grandchildren and great-grandchildren. Some of his stories are connected to one another, and some are not. Some are scary and some are funny. At the end of each story, Grandpa Christopher would play his guitar, and sing one of the songs he wrote to them. His offspring will jump, twirl, gallop, slap their thighs and butts, and box the air while mouthing words of the song. There's no special way of dancing to Grandpa's music, and all he wants to do is have fun with his offspring. Grandpa adores and cherishes this moment and will never trade it in for anything else.

Grandpa story is fiction

The Living Ghost

By

Blessing Abiaka

ONE

The Newspaper Ad

It's a bright and beautiful day in a quiet, middleclass suburban town. Cyclists, pedestrians and the occasional slow-rolling auto move harmoniously. A stylish jogger, 27-year-old, Joan Pastor, cuts down the sidewalk while listening her iPod. Joan maneuvers through a group of gawking men and women. One gave her a dirty look.

Joan comes to a sudden stop when she sees a newspaper on the ground. She turns off her iPod and then picks up the paper, which is folded to the classified ads. Joan's eyes immediately Catch two words printed in bold letters; "Roommate Needed." The words are large enough to be reflected in Joan's sunglasses. She pulls her cellphone from her pocket, and then dials the number on the ad.

"Hello? May I speak to Mr. Joey Noel? Hi Joey, my name is Joan Pastor. I'm responding to the ad you placed in the Metro Republic this morning. Are you still looking for a roommate?"

"Yes."

"That's great. Hold on, please," says Joan. She borrows a pen from a businessman sitting in front of a café with pastor, Ms. Mable Wright.

Joan continues. "I'm now ready to write down your information. And I'm happy to hear that there's still vacancy," Joan says. "How much is the rent?"

"It's $500 a month," Joey says. "Is it within your budget?"

"Yes. $500 is okay," Joan replies grimly.

"Good." Joey is happy.

Joan writes the rent amount in large numbers on the front of the paper and circles it. She gives the pen back to the businessman as three women stare at her, smiling, as they walk by.

"When are you coming to see the house?" Joey asks.

"That's not necessary," Joan replies.

"Why?" Joey asks.

"I already know the location. As it turns out, I had a girlfriend who used to live there, and I visited her all the time. It's a really nice place."

"Yes, it's nice." Joey is flabbergasted.

"Well, if you turn out to be a nice person, I'll move in immediately."

"Great, see you soon," Joey says. Her reaction puts the wrong idea into his head that she might be desperate to find a place.

"Bye-bye now," Joan says. She then turns around to thank the businessman who gave her the pen.

"Hey, young lady, what's your name?" the businessman asks.

Joan just looks at him, smiles, and then continues jogging.

The next day, Joan makes up her mind to move in with Joey. She gathers her belongings from the tiny studio she's renting from an elderly man, and then drives to check Joey out. Soon, she pulls up to a nice two-story home with a private fence surrounding the backyard. As she walks up the driveway, she notices the house has three car garages. The front door is propped open with some moving boxes, and she can hear loud music coming from inside. She knocks, but the music is too loud, and as a result Joey did not hear the knock on the door. So she cautiously enters the house.

Joan maneuvers through the boxes and comes into the living room, which is connected to the kitchen.

Joan removes her sunglasses. She is stunned that the home is in disarray. Boxes are everywhere, some are open and some are on their side with the contents spilling out. Suddenly, she hears a crash coming from the guest bathroom. Instinctively, she begins moving towards the crash, but then stops. "Hello. Is anyone here?"

Joan's voice is drowned out by the music. "Hello. Is anyone here?" She sighs and storms over to lower the stereo, dodging boxes along the way. She comes close to the stereo and stares at it for a moment. She then exhales loudly and pulls the plug out of the wall. Another strange sound comes from the bathroom. Joan can tell by the sounds that there's something there trying to get out. She trembles, and reluctantly drops the plug from her shaky hand.

The door to the bathroom flies open. Joey Noel stumbles out, tripping over two boxes. Joan gasps and places her back against the wall to catch him, but fails.

Joey looks up at Joan from the floor.

"Hi," Joan smiles at him.

He quickly gets up and leans against the wall. "Wow!"

She stares at him. "I'm Joan, Joan Pastor." She helps Joey regain his stance.

"Um, I'm here about the…remember, I talked to you on the phone."

"The room…Yeah, I know. I'm Joey," he introduces himself. "I don't fall quite often, but when I do, it's impressive."

Joan giggles. "Yeah, like my grandfather said, it's good to fall once in a while."

"Your grandfather said that? He must be a great man?" Joey teases her.

Joan laughs. "Yes, he was unique in his own little way," she acknowledges.

Joey dusts his hands off and reaches out to shake Joan's hand.

Joey turns and scans the living room. "So... this is the place. Is it like you remember when your friend lived here?"

"Well, it was more organized then, but basically the same."

"That's funny. I'm just moving in," Joey whispers.

Seeing the boxes scattered all over the place, Joan knew he was just moving in.

"I just came from Marry-Cruz about three weeks ago on a transfer," he says. "My company sent me here to set up a new branch office in Bull Moose."

Joan nods. "So, you mean you're not always a pack rat? Well, I'm glad to hear that because I was getting a little disappointed with the way things look in this room."

"I'm not a pack rat. I will have these boxes out of here in a day or two, I promise," Joey says.

"I'd like to see my room now if that's okay with you. Do you have boxes there too?"

"Actually, your room is the only room in the house that remains completely box free. It's impressive," Joey laughs. "I know you are well organized. I like that about you."

"You barely know me," Joan responds.

Joey escorts Joan upstairs.

"I don't really do well with disorganized people, no offense," he says. "I'm very organized in my own way. If you know what I mean."

They reached the top of the stairs.

"Please don't misunderstand me. I didn't say you're disorganized," he says, regretfully. "I barely know you."

"That's what I said. You barely know me. Yeah, you are weird," Joan mutters.

Joey walks Joan to the door of her room, and then moves boxes out of the way in order to open the door.

Joan leans over and looks into the room. "So you say you're from Marry-Cruz?" she asks him.

"That's right. That's my home."

Joan stares at him for a moment. "Me too, I'm from Marry-Cruz. I think this arrangement is going to work. There's no doubt about it."

Joey is shocked. "Are you? What a small world."

"Yes. Small world indeed," Joan says politely.

Joey and Joan head back to the living room.

"Do you like it here?" Joan asks.

"Actually, I do," Joey replies grimly. "It's a nice change of scenery."

Downstairs, Joan sits on the arm of the sofa—as Joey continues to go through some of his boxes. "Since we're going to be sharing a house, I think we should lay out some of the ground rules," Joan says

"Ground rules?" Joey is surprised.

"Yes, grounds rules," Joan sputters. "You know what I mean. The do's and don'ts." She tries to make a point.

"Okay, I'm listening."

"Please stay away from my room," Joan warns him.

Joey stops and looked at her.

"No offense," she explains. "It's just that I'm a private person, and I don't like people going through my stuff, or getting into my business."

"That's understandable," he is furious. "How do you know I want you as a roommate?"

"I'm never late with half of the rent, and I'm always punctual," she says proudly.

"I don't know that. I barely know you," Joey says.

"Take me by my word," Joan whispers.

Joey rubs his throat, and then stares at her. "I need one simple favor from you."

"What is it?" Joan asks, smiling.

"Do not bring in a candle in this house."

She stares at him. "Why not? Candles are romantic."

"Not to me," Joey says. "I hate the funky smell."

"Well, I'll respect your wish, if that's what you want," Joan promises.

"Yes, that's my wish. I'm glad it's okay with you."

"Well, since we have decided to be roommates. We have to compromise with each other," she exclaims.

Joey screams. "Roommates." The two shout and jump around the living room. "Roommate, roommate, roommate!"

"See you tomorrow,'" Joan waves at him, and heads towards the front door.

"See you tomorrow," Joey says and waves back at her.

TWO

Joan is Officially Joey's Roommate

Joan arrives at Joey's house with a small U-Haul attached to her car. She has boxes and other household items stored in the back of her car seat. After unloading her stuff from her car, she heads to the house carrying some boxes. Joey meets her at the bottom of the stairs and takes the boxes from her.

Joan is grateful. "Thanks, I really appreciate you helping me with my junk."

Joey stares at her. "Don't mention it. We're roommates now. We have to help each other out." Because the boxes were so heavy, Joey moves quickly and reaches the top of the stairs. Joan is right behind him.

Joey walks into Joan's room and sits the boxes down on her dresser.

Joan enters the room.

Joey looks around the room. "I know this is

the last time I'll be allowed into this room."

"Don't be silly, you're more than welcome to come in here—anytime I need something moved, or when there's bug that needs to be killed."

"Are you serious? You can't kill a bug?" Joey smiles, and walks out of the room.

At exactly 7 PM, Joan comes into the living room, and leaves the front door wide open. Exhausted, she drops down on the sofa. She looks around for Joey, but he's not in the room. She reaches for the TV remote on the coffee table, and turns on the TV.

"Joey, Joey, where are you?" she yells. "Guess what? I'm officially your roommate."

There's no response. She turns off the television, and then turns it back on again. She gets up, and heads for the kitchen. She walks over to the refrigerator and looks around the freezer. She reaches in and pulls out a Hot Pocket. Joan yells at Joey again. "I'm starving, so I'm eating one of your Hot Pockets, I hope you don't mind?"

There's no response. Joan closes the refrigerator and throws the Hot Pocket into the microwave. Smiling, she puts a hand to her ear—yelling out Joey's name. "Joey, where are you?" she asks. "If you don't want me to have one of your Hot Pockets, just say so."

No response. Her Hot Pocket finishes cooking and she grabs it and walks back into the living room. She sits down on the couch and places her snack on the table, and then takes a sip of juice from her cup. She is taking a bite of her snack, when suddenly she hears loud music from upstairs. Joan startled, drops the Hot Pocket on the rug. "What a mess!" she shouted. She quickly grabs the Hot Pocket, puts it back on her plate, and then she grabs a napkin to wipe the rug.

"Oh, God, I'm going nuts. I'm destroying the place already," she says to herself. "I have to get it together."

The music from upstairs continued, and then she hears Joey singing along horribly off-key. Joan sighs loudly and sits back down. As the music gets louder, she becomes irritated. "Oh, Lord, what have I got myself into?"

Joan grabs her plate, takes another sip from her cup, and heads back into the kitchen to wash her plate. Exactly 9 PM, she went to her bedroom to sleep.

In the morning, Joan comes out of her room wearing a robe with a bath towel draped over her shoulder. She walks over to the bathroom door and reaches for the door knob. As she tries to open the door, she hears the sound of the shower running. Joan sighs, and walks back to her room, and sits on her bed. Her eyes travel, and she notices that it's 8:45 AM. She turns on the TV, and lies down.

After a while she looks back at the clock. "Gosh, it's 9:45 AM." She gets out of bed, and with her towel, heads for the bathroom. At the bathroom door, she still hears the sound of the running water. Joan, annoyed, knocks on the door.

"Hey, Joey, do you mind if I take a shower while we have some water left?"

There was no response.

She knocks harder. "Joey!"

No response, but she can hear Joey singing in the shower.

Joan, angry that Joey is spending too much time in the bathroom, yells at him. "Joey, if you don't come out of there right now, I will break this door down!"

The singing stopped, but no one responded.

"Joey, what are you doing there?" she shouted. "I had no idea you were such a girl."

When there is no response, Joan kicks the door.

Joey peeks out from his room. "Joan, what's the matter with you? You are a little loud this morning."

Joan spins around and gasps, she sees Joey leaning out of his room, two doors down.

"I didn't see... I mean, I didn't see......"

"Joan, I don't know what you're talking about," Joey says. "Why are you kicking the door?"

"I was tired of waiting for you to come out of the bathroom."

Joey steps out of his room, only wearing boxers. "You woke me up. Why are you mad at the bathroom door?"

"Someone has been in this bathroom for nearly two hours," she replies. "The shower has been running and the door is locked."

Joey, shocked, stares at Joan.

"Who is in the bathroom?" she asks. "Do you have company? The water is still running."

"I didn't have any company last night," Joey says.

Joey walks over to the bathroom door, and leans to place his ear on the door. "Joan, the water is not running."

"I know what I heard Joey. I even heard you singing in there," Joan says. "If no one is in there, then why is the door locked?" Joan opens the bathroom door. Amazed, she steps back.

"Hello?" She slowly enters the bathroom with Joey a step behind her.

Joey walks over to the bathtub, and sticks his hand in the tub.

Joan stares at him.

He looks up at Joan. "The tub is dry, Joan," Joey says.

Joan looks around the room as she pulls her robe tighter.

"Are you ok?" he asks. "There's no one here."

"Someone was in here. I know what I heard," she argues. "Joey, seriously, someone was in the bathroom this morning."

"Maybe you're just... "

"Maybe I'm what?" Joan asks.

"Crazy," Joey laughs out loud. He pats Joan on the shoulder and walks out of the bathroom, laughing in the hallway.

Joan yells at him. "You're rude and mean!" She slams the door.

"It's sad you're stuck with me, Joan. For 12 whole months," Joey says. "I shouldn't have let you sign a contract for a whole year. Now, I know that I made a grievous mistake. You're going to burn me out."

On Friday evening, Joan is coming down the stairs. She goes through the living room, and makes her way towards the kitchen. A large humanoid shadow appears on the wall. Joan, trembling, gasps and quickly turns around to see what is casting it, but there's nothing there. She takes a moment to scan the entire downstairs.

"Okay, girl, get yourself together," she mumbles to herself. She turns back to the wall, and the shadow is gone. She's terrified. "Whatever you are—I want you out of this house," she says to the shadow. "You are freaking me out."

The next morning, Joan wakes up. She walks into the kitchen to make herself a cup of coffee. The pot is a quarter-full of coffee from the night before. She sighs and opens the cabinet, pulling out a fresh filter and the coffee canister. Joan turns back to the coffeemaker, and accidentally drops the coffee and the filter. Disappointed, she stares at a pot of what appears to be a fresh brewing coffee. She reaches out and touches the pot. It's hot. She burns her finger. Perplexed, she touches the pot again. It's still hot. She shrugs and proceeds to fill her cup, anyway.

Joey dressed in a suit and tie enters the kitchen. He observes the spilled coffee and sees Joan staring at the coffeemaker. "Are you having problems with the coffeemaker?" he asks.

Joan shivers. "What?"

"Why are you staring at the coffee pot?" Joey puts his briefcase on the counter, and then goes to the pantry to find a broom. "What happened here? Did you drop the coffee on the floor?" Joey begins to clean up the coffee.

"I don't know what is wrong with me," Joan mutters. "I think I'm just spacing. I've gone through so many changes in one week, with the move and other minor things. I can't even make a pot of coffee."

"I know how it is," Joey tries to cheer her up. "You think you can be kind enough to make me a cup? Dump lots of sugar in it. I love it when it's hot and sweet."

"Oh, sure. Thanks for cleaning my mess."

Joey goes over and gets a big coffee mug out of the cabinet, and hands it over to Joan.

"Are you thinking of staying up late today?" Joan asks him. "It's just morning."

She got him confused. "What are you talking about?" He frowned.

"You made coffee for more than 10 people this morning," she replies. "We're only two in this house."

Joey dumps the spilt coffee in the trash. "What do you mean?"

"You made the coffee this morning, didn't you?" she asked. "That's too much coffee for the both of us. We're two in this house."

Joey sips his coffee. "I didn't make the coffee, I thought you did. It's good."

Joan looks at him. "Why do you have to lie so much?"

"Excuse me?" Joey's' face turns red.

"You lied about being in the bathroom a couple of days ago. Now it's the coffee."

"It seems you're a little cranky this morning," Joey says. He goes across the table, and picks his briefcase. "This argument is going too far. I know when to back off from an argument— and I'm backing off right now!" He stares at her. "You are a nagger, but I still think you're cool."

Joan flips. "Don't do that. Don't patronize me. I'm not crazy. There are only two of us living in this house, Joey," Joan sputtered. "If I'm not in the bathroom, or making coffee, that only leaves you; unless there's an extremely clean, caffeine-loving ghost among us."

Joey takes a deep breath. "Listen to me carefully; I did not make the coffee," he said strongly. "I'm out of here. I hope you're in better spirits by the time I get home." Joey goes out of the back door.

Joan walks back into the kitchen, and glances at the coffee maker.

THREE

The Study Hall

Joan and her two classmates, Thelma William and Phil Greg, were sitting in the living room. Phillip is the youngest among them. Thelma is a year or two younger than Joan, but likes to dress like an older lady.

The group is studying, and hovering about open textbooks. There are three cups of decaf coffee on the table next to Philip.

"I am not getting any of this," Joan admits.

"I like Mr. Durant assignments. I think he's a cool guy," Phil tells them—as he takes off his eyeglasses. He uses his sweater to clean it. He raises his head, and stares at Joan. "All you have to do is pay attention to his voice fluctuations in class to know what information to write down."

"That's the problem. His tests are based on his lectures and not on the text," she expressed concern. "Why in the world are we forced to pay for these expensive text-books if he's not going to make use of them?" Joan reaches over and takes a sip of her coffee. "I have a short attention span. I can't focus in his classroom. Blah, blah, blah, fluctuation, blah, blah, blah."

Thelma and Phillip laughs at her.

"Now, you can see why I'm failing," Joan says.

"Why don't you get a tape recorder?" Thelma asks Joan. "I think I have an extra one at home. I'll lend it to you."

"I'll appreciate that, thank you," Joan replies.

Phil is getting tired. He leans forward and pulls his textbook closer to him. "Okay, ladies, let's see who gets this one. How many countries are in Africa?"

Thelma laughs. "You know, that reminds me of something my grandmother said sometime last week."

Joan frowns. "Who cares about what your grandmother said?"

Phillip sighs and lowers the book.

Thelma laughs. "Joan, I know you don't want to hear what my grandmother said, but I'll say it anyway," she said. "My grandmother was watching a show about Africa. I asked her which country in Africa? And she kept on saying the same thing 'Africa, child, 'Africa.' I told her

Africa is a continent, not a country."

Joan smiles. "Your grandmother is not the only one. So many people cannot tell the difference between a country and a continent."

Phil gets up from his seat. "This grandma story is making me sleepy," he says. "This coffee is not keeping me up. Joan, please make me stronger coffee."

There are two different pots of coffee brewing in the kitchen. One pot has a black cover, and the other one has a pink cover. The pot with a pink cover is decaffeinated coffee—while the pot with black cover is a regular coffee. Since he poured the coffee for himself—Joan wants to know where he got the coffee from.

"No wonder it tastes funky," Phil said. "I got it from the pink pot."

"That's why you're falling asleep," Joan laughed at Phillip. "You're drinking decaffeinated coffee."

Thelma cracks up.

"Who made the decaffeinated coffee?" Phillip asks. "I know for sure you drink the regular one."

"Joey made it. Once in a while he dilutes the regular coffee with decaffeinated coffee," Joan explained.

Phillip walks into the kitchen to make himself another cup of coffee.

"Hey, Thelma, let's forget your grandma's story and talk about something else," Joan says.

Thelma grabs a napkin from the table, balls it up and throws it at Joan.

Phil howls from the kitchen. "Thelma, would you like a cup of coffee? I can make you one."

"No, sir," Thelma replies quickly. "I'm not a coffee person. Half a cup keeps me awake for five days."

Joan laughs. She gets off the couch, and stares at the door leading to the kitchen. She pauses, and then remembers the shadow that passed by her in the morning. Trembling, she drops her cup of coffee and it shatters on the floor.

Phillip and Thelma look up.

"Joan," Phillip calls her.

"Joan, are you okay?" Thelma gets up and goes over to her. "Joan."

Joan turns and looks at Thelma, as if she's noticing her presence for the first time.

"Joan," Thelma calls again.

"I'm…" Joan stops.

Thelma escorts Joan back to the couch. "You must be exhausted. We can go ahead and call it off for the day."

"Sorry, something just crossed my mind. I think you're right, I'm getting tired."

"It's not a problem, Joan. We'll just catch up with you tomorrow in our usual lunch room," Phillip tries to cheer Joan up.

Joan puts on a fake smile and walks them to the door.

FOUR

The Hidden Voices

Joan is sleeping in her bed, when soft voices come from nowhere in the dark. They get louder and eventually wake Joan up. She turns over and grabs the alarm clock from the nightstand. "You've got to be kidding?" Joan said angrily. She kicks the comforter off of her—and slides out of bed and into some house shoes. She slip into her robe and heads for the door.

Joan slightly opens the door of her bedroom, and peeks through her door. She can clearly hear voices laughing and carrying on downstairs. She stumbles to the edge of the stairway. All she can see is the bright light reflecting off the floor downstairs.

She yells, "Joey, could you guys please keep it down? It's 1: AM. I've a test tomorrow, I need to sleep!"

The noise settles down a little bit, and Joan

turns around to go back to sleep in her room.

As she sleeps, the voices rise up again. She turns over and picks up the alarm clock from the nightstand. "I think Joey is trying my patience again."

Joan kicks off the covers, and slides out of bed again and into some house shoes. This time she forgets the robe and heads out her bedroom door. She stops at the top of the stairway, and gapes. The lights are still bright. She yells, "You guys get to run every single light down there?"

The voice gets louder this time.

Joan, bitter, rushes down the stairs and as her feet touch the floor all the lights goes out. She pauses. "This isn't funny guys." She moves a step forward from the stairs, and yells out her roommate's name. "Joey!"

The voices fall silent. The only lights shining in the room are the ones coming from the street lamps outside the window. The lights cast an eerie feel in the room.

"Hello? Hello?"Joan comes around the corner and peers into the living room. She slides her hand up and down the wall. Finally, she finds the light switch and flips it on. The room is completely empty.

Joan scans the entire room. There's no trace of anyone. She's hearing people giggling around the kitchen. Joan dashes over to the kitchen and flips the lights. It's empty. She goes to the back door and peers out of the window. The porch light cuts on and Joan pulls the curtain back slightly. She can't see anyone out there either. She stays in the darkness for few minutes, and then closes the curtain.

Joan moves away from the back door and comes to the garage door. She opens the garage door slightly, and looks inside. Nothing. She moves towards the living room and pauses as she hears people whispering.

"Shh! Shh! Shh! She's coming."

Joan freaks out. She looks around the dark living room. The curtains are now closed. She fumbles for the light switch, but the lights won't turn back on. She starts to cry. Her heartbeat rises, and she starts breathing fast. Suddenly, she gets dizzy and slides down the wall to the floor.

Joan moans and screams. She feels strange screaming so loudly, but she continues. Joey runs into the living room.

Joan cling's her arms around him.

"What's the matter?" Joey asks.

"You...you won't believe me."

Joey pulls her close to the couch. "Of course I will," he says. "Just tell me what's going on."

"I overheard people talking and laughing in the living room. I thought you had some friends over. I came down to ask you to keep it down." She pauses, trying to catch her breath.

Joey rubs her back until she calms down.

"But there was nobody in here. The lights…the lights were on, and then they were off."

Joey stares at Joan. He slightly pulls away from her.

"They were whispering—shhh,shhh she is coming."

Joey stands up, and paced up and down the room. "I didn't sign up for this, you know. Joan, you got a problem. I mean the kind of problem that only a psychiatrist can help you with. You're sick."

Joan gets to her feet. "Shut up! I'm not sick, Joey. I know what I heard."

"Joan, you're hearing things—you're seeing things. Me, nothing!" he said. "I've seen nothing. So I'm going back to my same little room and to my same little bed."

Joey heads for the stairs. Half way down he turns around and looks at Joan. "You better believe it I'm locking my door."

Joan rushes over and grabs Joey's right arm. "You are staying here."

Joey pauses. "Are you serious?"

She stares at the ceiling. "I've never been more serious in my life."Joan guides Joey over to the couch. She eases him down and sits next to him.

She curls up next to Joey and clings to his arm. She lays her head on a pillow he had left on the couch, earlier.

Joey perturbed by her actions speaks out. "This isn't what I had in mind."

The next day, Joan is in the kitchen washing dishes. She hears someone come in through the front door. She dried her hands with a towel before entering the living room. She looks towards the front door, but no one is there. She heads back to the kitchen. Ten minutes later, she hears someone call her name. "Joan!"

Joan turns back, and then screams.

There's an unnaturally tall figure standing a few feet right in front of her. She is not seeing the figure. The figure is wearing a long black robe and a white mask.

Joan, terrified, scans the room. "Is…is anyone there?" She stammers as she looks around. Since she doesn't see anyone, she thinks the room is empty, but the large figure starts to move towards the stairs.

Joan can hear the sound of wood creaking as the figure's steps lure her to the stairs. Joan follows the steps and stops at the base and looks upward. There are no lights upstairs.

The figure in black is barely visible at the top of the stairs. She hears another voice calling her name. "Joan."

Two minutes later, someone sneezes in the kitchen. "Joey, is that you?" she asks.

No one responds.

Joan does not see anyone in the kitchen. "Joey, you are a miserable son of a bitch! I know it's you."

She raises her head, and sees a lamp fly from the living room's end table and crash onto the floor. Joan freezes. She then approaches the shattered lamp, and looks over it. Suddenly, the broken pieces scatter and slam into the surrounding walls and the floor boards, breaking into smaller pieces. The cover of the lamp whips around Joan's leg.

She screams and stumbles backwards to the floor, and she starts to cry.

The figure looms over her, and he bends in an unnatural curve. A light fog pours from beneath his robe. Still, she is seeing no one.

She hears another voice yelling at her name. "Jooooooaaaaaaannnnnnnnnnnn!

"Are you a ghost?" she asks, and starts to rise from the floor. "You are, aren't you?"

The voice starts to laugh.

"Hahahahahahahahahahahhhahahah!"

Joan summons the courage to back away

from the laughter. She can't remember hearing any stories of ghosts talking and laughing like human being.

As she contemplates, she hears the footsteps coming towards her. Joan jumps to her feet and dashes to the kitchen as her breath hardens. She proceeds to grab a large knife from the counter. She turns around and raises the knife, ready for a battle. "Come any closer, and I'll kill you." The dark figure is standing directly in front of her. Joan's eyes dart from left to right looking for any sign of it.

After a moment, Joan's breathing is under control. She slowly lowers the knife and places it on the top of the counter—then she rushes out of the kitchen, runs upstairs and into her bedroom. The dark figure stands beside her door.

Joan opens the drawer, and starts sorting her clothes to get them ready for laundry.

The dark figure zooms beside her. Joan feels his energy. She picks up a hand gun, and spins around with it. She points the gun in every direction, all over her room. Her heartbeat rises again, and her chest heats up. She could feel the dark figure's energy all over her room. "Don't you come near me, whatever you are," Joan warns whatever it is. She continues to point the gun in different directions. "Are you listening?

Stay away from me. I have a gun, and I'm not afraid to use it."

There is no response, but she refuses to drop her gun. She starts to move away from the dresser. "I wish I could see your ugly face."

Then she hears the sounds of breaking glasses coming from downstairs—and sounds of folks, spoons and plates. "Someone is eating in the kitchen." Joan flies down the stairs. She swings around the corner and sees no one—but the coffee table has been kicked over, and its glass lay shattered on the floor.

Joan starts to panic again. She bounces around the living room with the gun leading her way.

Suddenly, footsteps begin to run towards her. She points the gun and shoots.

Then she screams. "Stay away from me!" Joan closes her eyes and empties the chamber. She lowered the weapon. It falls onto the center table, and shattered the glass. She withers onto the couch. "A big mess," she said, and lay on the couch for about twenty minutes. When she's up, she walks into the guest bathroom—about to close the door—she hears the toilet flushing and water running by itself.

Frightened, she runs out of the guest bathroom. Outside the door, she looks up and stops in her tracks. The shattered tables and glasses are now intact again—like nothing happened. The broken lamps are unbroken, but the gun was gone.

From a distance she sees a pair of men's shoes and a pack of cigarettes on the coffee table. She goes to the coffee table and picks up the shoes and examines them. "These are Joey's," Joan says, and her eyes widen. "Oh my God! He's home."

Joan goes to the bottom of the stairs. "Joey? Joey? Are you here?"

There's no response.

"Joey, please answer me."

Joan then feels hands around her neck. She can't see anyone, but she can feel the hands. "Please…please don't. Please don't kill me," she begged for her life.

The hands release Joan, and she falls to the floor crying. She makes her way to the door and crawls out of the house.

FIVE

Joan Meets Pastor Wright

Pastor Mable Wright, of the Christian Church pulls into the driveway. She's a decent looking woman in her early fifties. She parks her car and walks across the street to check her mailbox. She pulls out some letters and starts going through them, and then something catches her eyes across the street.

Joan is stumbling, and perambulating up and down the street. She looks weak and disconnected.

Pastor Wright places the mail back into the mailbox, and starts walking towards Joan. She approaches Joan with a caution. Joan doesn't seem to notice her. "Young lady, how are you doing?"

Joan continues walking.

Pastor Wright stands in her path. "Are you alright?" she asks, fiercely.

"Huh?" Joan replies absentmindedly.

"I asked if you are alright. I'm Mable Wright," she informs her. "I noticed you pacing up and down the street. You seem a little distressed. By the way I'm a pastor."

Joan looks up. "How did I end up here," she asks herself.

"Are you running from something," Pastor Wright asks.

Joan stares at her. "I don't know what I'm doing on the street." Joan starts to cry again.

Pastor Wright places a hand on her shoulder. "Do you live around here?"

"I live a few blocks away," Joan replies.

Pastor Wright gasps and suddenly yanks her hand away from Joan. "Your soul is troubled. I sensed that you're in danger," says the pastor.

Joan looks at Pastor Wright for the first time. "How did you know?"

"I'm a psychic."

"Can you pray for me?" Joan requests.

"Yes, but do you want to do this right here on the street?" Pastor Wright asks her.

Joan looks around. "Do you mind coming to my house and praying with me there?"

"I can pray anywhere, anytime. God said we can call upon his name anytime anywhere," Pastor Wright puts an arm around Joan's shoulder, and escorts her to her car.

Joan and Pastor Wright enter the house. Joan hears a noise in the kitchen, and she heads to that direction with the pastor. Inside the kitchen, they see Joey leaning on the counter eating an apple and reading a newspaper. He is surprised to see Joan with a woman in oversized clothing. Pastor Mable Wright always wears oversized clothes.

Joey without looking up talks to Joan. "I thought I saw you going for a walk a while ago." He takes another bite of his apple.

"When did you come back?" Joan asks, furiously.

Joey is still looking down at the paper. "I was here a few minutes ago." He says hello to Pastor Wright.

Pastor Wright takes a deep breath and grips her purse tightly. She holds Joan on her arm and leads her towards the living room. Half way down the living room, she stops but allows Joan to continue going. "I would like to talk to the guy in the kitchen," she tells Joan.

Joey, still looking at the paper saw Pastor Wright staring at him. "Don't look at me that way," he scolded her.

Pastor Wright gasps again and hurries out of the kitchen. She didn't like what she saw. "I will be back," Pastor Wright says, and leaves the house.

The pastor returns an hour later. This time, Joan is sitting on the couch inside the living room, resting her head in her hands.

Pastor takes a sit beside Joan, but she's not paying attention to Joan, she's facing the kitchen looking at Joey.

Joey turns around and smirks at Pastor Wright. "You don't have a home to go to?" he asks, rudely.

Pastor Wright jumps up from the chair. "I don't take nonsense from anyone, young man."

Joey gets up from his seat and heads toward the living room. "Excuse me?"

Pastor Wright puts her hands on her hips "You heard me! What's the matter?" the pastor asked him. "Do you feel threatened by me?"

Joan stands up.

Joey ignores Joan.

"How dare you speak to me that way?" Joey asks, bitterly. "You don't know me."

Pastor Wright walks across the room, and picks up the shoes off the coffee table. She walks back to Joan. "Joan, whose shoes are these?"

"They must be Joey's, although I don't know how they got there," Joan mutters. "I went to the bathroom and when I came out, they were there."

Pastor Wright stares at Joey. She closes her eyes and squeezes the shoes. She takes a deep breath and slowly opens her eyes. When she does she is looking directly at Joey. "Joey, are these yours?" she asks, strangely.

"No," Joey replies, grimly.

Pastor Wright throws the shoes at Joey's feet. He hops backwards to avoid them.

"Hey!" Joey yelled at Pastor Wright.

"Don't lie to me. Those are your shoes. I see them on your feet," Pastor Wright scolded Joey.

Joey kicks the shoes aside. "What are you talking about?" he asked. "Those shoes are not on my feet." He was angry at Joan for inviting a stranger into the house.

"She's a psychic, Joey. She knows you don't have them on you, now, but she knows you've worn them before," Joan explains.

Pastor Wright walks closer to Joey. "So can you tell me how your shoes came to be on this coffee table?"

Joey turns and storms off towards the stairs.

Pastor Wright turns and grabs her purse. She takes Joan by the arm, and they walk towards the front door. "There are lots of activities going on in the house, child. Go get some incense and burn them night and day."

Joey rushes downstairs. He stops in front of Joan. "You are not bringing incense or candles in

-to this house. I can't stand the smell. Do you un-derstand me?"

Pastor Wright steps between the two of th-em and faces Joey. "So you're afraid of poor old ladies and incense, huh?"

"Joan, I'm serious. I can't stand the smell of incense," he said. "Don't bring any into this house." Joey turns and goes back up stairs.

Pastor Wright looks at Joan. "I've to leave, child. I'll pray for you when I get home."

Joan stands there watching Pastor Wright walk down the road and to her car. As soon as the car pulls out of the driveway, Joan turns to Joey. "What was that all about?"

Joey turns and heads to the stairs. "I hate her."

"Why?" Joan asks. "You don't know her."

SIX

The Cats & The Robed Figure

Joan is home alone, one afternoon, studying for her final exam in the upstairs den with open text books and papers scattered all over the center table. As she works on her laptop, she is also busy eating potato chips. She drinks from a soda can, scratches her left hand, and then walks down the hallway into the bathroom.

When Joan returns to the den she notices that the table has been moved to the left hand corner of the room, and her books are scattered on the floor. She scans the room, leans back, and looks down the hall at Joey's room. His door is still closed and the lights are out.

Joan shrugs and walks over to the desk. "I know you're in here."

The dark figure hides behind a sofa. The figure points towards a book and flings it against the wall.

Joan jumps, but quickly composes herself. "You may as well come out and let me see you. I won't let you scare me anymore."

She takes a deep breath and reaches for her soda can and takes a long drink. Suddenly, she hears cracking sounds coming from the coffee table, but the glass is not breaking. The table begins to shake.

"Did you hear me? I won't let you scare me anymore. I refuse to live in fear because of you. I wish you'll have the courage to come out here and let me see who you are." Joan starts to laugh at what she is saying to the dark figure harassing her. She wonders if whatever it is heard her.

The house phone starts to ring. She slowly walks to the activity center to answer the phone. "So you are going to call me instead, huh? This better not be long distance." She picks up the phone. "Hello? Are you there?"

No answer.

Joan continues, "Helloooo!"

No answer.

Joan hangs up the phone and looks around the room. "This is very strange," she says. She dumps the receiver on the coffee table, and grabs her laptop and sits back down. "Stop moving that damn desk back and forth!" she yells at whatever it is.

Joan studies for another hour then heads downstairs. She's one hundred percent sure that Joey is nowhere in the house, so she nervously pulls incense from the bag, and fumbles around her pocket for a lighter. She finds the lighter and leans forward to light the incense, but a breeze comes from nowhere and blows the flame out from the lighter.

Joan turns around and saw Joey standing over her.

"What are you doing?" Joey asks, angrily.

Joan is surprised to see Joey. "Joey, how did you get in here?"

"I asked you a question first," Joey retorts.

"I checked your room. You were not there. Where did you come from?"

Joey throws his hand in the air. "Damn it, Joan! I walked. Okay? I walked in and I saw you messing around with incense."

Joey starts pacing up and down the room. "I don't know what that pastor has been telling you, but you are not well. You've been losing it for a while now, you need to see someone. That pastor is not helping you!"

Pastor Wright comes in from nowhere. "Are you sure?" she asks Joey.

Joan and Joey turn around to see Pastor Wright standing in the living room with them.

"Hello, Joan," Pastor Wright greets her.

"Okay, now where did you come from?" Joey asks.

"A wide open door is an invitation for company," Pastor Wright replies. She walks across the room and takes a seat in one of the chairs. She tells Joey not to change the subject. "You claim that Joan needs to see a psychiatrist, I think you're the one that need help."

"She's the one hearing voices," Joey explained

"She didn't have that problem before, until she came to live with you." Pastor Wright changes her seat, and places her right hand on the edge of the couch. "Tell me something. Joey, do you believe in God?"

"Are you trying to say that everything she's going through is somehow my fault?" he asks, furiously.

Pastor Wright smiles, "You said that, not me."

Joey throws a fit. "Oh my God! Both of you are crazy." He turns to walk out of the room, but looks back at the women. "Joan, get some help."

Joey points towards Pastor Wright. "And you lady! You'll never see me in your church," he shoots her a conspiracy look and leaves the room.

Pastor Wright fires back, screaming at him. "You're not welcome there. In my church we

44

don't look for the dead among the living!" The pastor gets up from her seat, grabs her handbag, and then turns to Joan. "Listen to me, child, before there was Abraham, there was Jesus. Look to Jesus child, not man. Don't forget to read your bible before going to bed in the night."

"I do read the bible at bedtime," Joan says, and walk the pastor to the front door.

"What'd you be doing when I leave?" Pastor Wright asks Joan.

"I'm going to do my laundry," Joan replies with a smile. "It's overdue."

"You do that, child," Pastor Wright says, and opens the door.

Joan, now inside her room gathers her dirty clothes and put them in two baskets. She carries the baskets to the laundry room, one at a time. While her clothes are in the washer and dryer, she studies for her exam in the den.

When the first load of laundry is done, Joan places it in the basket, and carries it up to her room. She stops at the door, and places the laundry basket down to open the door. She walks into her room with the basket, only to drop it and spill her clothes on the floor. She screams, and her heart pounded.

Joan is startled by the presence of six big cats lounging on her bed.

"Joey, come here!" she commanded him.

"What now?" Joey asks, reluctantly.

"There are six big cats in my room. You have to come see this."

"What?" Joey shook his head.

Joey runs upstairs. "Did you leave your windows open or something?" He takes a look around Joan's room, and bursts into laughter. Joey slams his hand hard against the door frame. "Where are they?"

"What?" Joan asks. She looks back into her room and there are no cats in sight. "I don't understand this, they were....."

"They were what? Sitting on your bed playing poker?"

Joan wants to talk back, but just folds her arms instead.

Joey is not amused. "Well, you just told me six cats were sitting on your bed. Where are they?"

"They must be hiding somewhere in the room," Joan is confused. "They were just there, I swear."

"What was I thinking? I just came running up the stairs for nothing."

Joan angry yells at Joey. "Stop it!"

"Crazy, crazy, crazy lady! She sees cats, she see bats!"

"Stop it. Stop it, Joey." She starts to cry.

"Joan, don't you get it, yet? Can't you see? Something in you has snapped," he tries to tell her how he feels about her seeing things and hearing stuff.

Joan pulls herself together. "Maybe they're in your room." She walks over to Joey's door and shakes his door knob.

"Hey, stop!"

Joan didn't stop. She violently continues to shake his door knob. "Why don't you open your door?"

"There's nothing in my room, Joan. For God's sake stop this!" Joey turns and walks towards the stairs.

Joan runs after him. "I am not delusional! There were cats in there. I'm not crazy. Pastor Wright doesn't think so."

Joey stops at the middle of the den when he spotted one of his pants lying on the floor near the laundry room.

Joan steps aback.

"Joan, those are my pant on the floor."

Joan looks at him directly in his face. "It must have fallen off the basket. I did your laundry."

He is stunned to hear that. "You're not supposed to," says Joey. "You did the same thing a month ago."

"I thought you needed a helping hand. The

47

laundry basket has been sitting in the laundry room for more than a week." Joan stares at him.

Joey thanks Joan for the help. "You're a wonderful person, but do yourself a favor and get some help." After talking to Joan, Joey starts walking towards the stairs. He stops to talk to her again.

"Pastor Wright is not helping you. She has been praying for you for over six months, and you're not getting any better. What you need is a psychological evaluation."

SEVEN

The Kitchen

Joan is busy cooking in the kitchen when the pot starts to overflow. She opens the lid half -way.

Joey walks into the kitchen, sniffing. "What are you cooking? It smells good."

Joan laughs. "What are you doing behind my back?" she asks. "You've been hiding there for more than five minutes."

"It smells nice."

"I asked you a question. What are you doing behind my back?" she frowns.

"What I'm doing is not illegal," Joey whispers. "I'm just watching you cook." He turns around and walks out of the kitchen.

"No offense," Joan says. She wipes her hands on a towel and follows him.

Joey enters the living room with Joan in tow. He turns on the television.

She stands beside Joey. "Okay, Joey, what

are you up to, now? You're acting weird."

"I didn't do anything illegal. All l did was to hide behind your back," Joey says. "Moreover, there's nothing wrong with being nice to my wonderful roommate."

"You are trying to be nice, how?" Joan asks. "You've been horrible to me lately. Just the other day you made me cry. You call me crazy all the time. Now you're acting crazy."

Joey looks at Joan. "I told you the simple truth. You need help. Calling you names doesn't mean I don't care about you."

Before Joan can reply, the door bell rings. She goes to the door and opens it. It is Edith Wells, who is a longtime friend of Joan's. She also teaches at the college where Joan attends school. Joan welcomes her into the house and leads her to the kitchen.

"Hi, Joey," Edith greets.

Joey waves at Edith and reaches for a magazine on the coffee table.

Joan and Edith enter the kitchen and sit beside the dining table. "Girl, whatever it is you are cooking smells wonderful. I am starving," Edith says.

Joan smiles. "No worries."

Joan looks in the cabinet and pulls out two plates and two glasses.

Joey tries to eavesdrop on the girls —but

they are quiet. He throws the magazine on the coffee table and heads upstairs, but stops halfway on the stairs.

Joan smiles at Edith.

"The last time I talked to you, you sounded hysterical," Edith mentions. "What's going on?"

"Strange things have been happening in this house," Joan responds. "It's becoming more and more frequent."

Joey loudly clears his throat from the stairs, which makes Joan jump and shiver.

Edith looks around, and she notices that Joey has left the living room. "Where did he go?"

"He's in the den—upstairs," Joan replies.

"Girl, strange things have been happening all over." Edith swallows.

Joan got the message Joey was trying to send, so she changes the subject and twists it a little bit. "Yeah, like those earthquakes hitting different countries."

"Yeah," Edith tries to back her story. "If is not one thing, it's the other."

"All these things were predicted in the Bible. But I don't think we're at the end of the world," Joan says.

Joey tries to come back to the living room to listen to the girls, but he quickly changes his mind and goes back upstairs.

"If you really know your bible, God said—

when strange things start to happen, the end is near," Edith says."

"Yeah, the bottom line is that the end of the world is drawing near," says Joan.

"The world is old," Edith adds. "Look at some of the structures that were made millions of years ago. They are barely standing."

The ladies take a break from the conversation, and eat their food silently.

After a little while, Edith gets up to leave. "Well, I have to get going. I still have an assignment due tomorrow," she says.

"Oh, I forget that you were taking a course. Are you going for your PhD?"

"Actually, I'm changing to medicine," Edith exclaims.

Joan escorts Edith to the front door. "No way! Good for you, girl. Go for it. Doctors are paid good money."

"Don't worry, girl, the money won't spoil me."

Joan cracks up. They hug each other. Edith opens the front door and leaves the house.

Joey walks down the stairs and goes into the kitchen. Joan follows him.

Joan, angry, scolds Joey. "You're vindictive. You humiliate me in front of my friends, you call me psycho, and I think you are crazier than me."

Inside the kitchen Joey opens the fridge and looks around it, while Joan leans against the counter.

"I feel like kicking your ass, right now. Why did you stop me from telling Edith about all the strange things I've seen in this house," Joan asks, furiously.

Joey closes the refrigerator and spins around. He grasps Joan's neck. "I actually enjoyed the little bullshit session you had there," Joey says. "I like Edith, I think she's smart."

Joan tries to wiggle away from Joey.

"Hey, hey, look at me," Joey says, gently.

Joan is still struggling to free herself from him.

"I applaud you for being understanding. Under no circumstances should you talk about any of these things going on in this house with your friends," Joey warns her seriously. He moves his hands from her neck to her waist.

"You know what, I think I'm starting to like you," Joey whispers. "I like women who like to argue."

"What's wrong with talking about the strange things to my friends?" Joan asks.

"Your friends won't understand. One by one, they will all desert you," Joey informs her. "They might think you are schizophrenic. Nothing breaks up a relationship like mental illness. I am telling the truth. I'm being serious here."

Joan stares at Joey for a moment, and then frees herself. "Close that mouth, Joey. You don't know what you're talking about. I'm not sick."

Joey turns around and scolds Joan. "I don't like the way you talk to me. I'm a man, I have big ego, so stop bringing me down!"

Joan walks towards Joey. "You'll be happy to know that I have an appointment with Dr. Ross tomorrow. He's a psychologist. He'll be here at 11 AM."

"Why is he coming to the house?" Joey asks. "You should go to his office."

"Because I feel more comfortable here than in an office," Joan responds.

"You know home visits are quite a bit expensive, right?"

"I know. Can I ask you a question?"

Joey turns towards the refrigerator. "Free country. What?"

Joan goes over behind Joey. "How come you don't look at people in the eyes? You never make eye contact with me," Joan mutters.

Joey turns around and stares at her for a moment, and then glides out of the kitchen.

EIGHT

The Mystery Stereo

Joan is sitting at the dining table doing her homework, when the stereo comes on by itself, it's playing the same music she heard when she first came to the house to meet Joey. Joan jumps and leaps to her feet, knocking her glass of water on the floor.

She slowly walks to the stereo to turn it off, but stops to listen to the music. She starts to sway back and forth and mouth the words to the song. Soon, she is dancing around the living room. The house phone starts to ring. Joan goes back to the stereo to turn it down, but as soon as her hand is near the volume control, the stereo stops by itself. Joan shrugs and heads to answer the phone. That's when the music comes back on, louder than before. The music is so loud that Joan has to cover her ears. She tries again to turn down the volume, but the volume stays the same.

Joan begins pushing buttons at random, but nothing seems to be working. The phone continues to ring. Joan turns around to look at the phone, and then continues working on the stereo.

Frustrated, she hits the stereo, and then picks it up and shakes it. The phone continues to ring. She puts the stereo back on the entertainment center, and rushes over to the phone. The music cuts off as she nears the phone, but it turns back on, full blast, when Joan picks up the telephone receiver. Joan sticks a finger in her ear.

"Hello?" It's Pastor Wright. "Hi, Pastor. I think so. Yes, Dr. Ross will be here tomorrow at 11 AM," Joan says. "Yeah, I know it's loud."

Joan moves back towards the stereo. The Dark Figure is standing by the stereo watching Joan.

"I can't turn the music down." Joan yells. "Yeah, Pastor Wright, I know what you are talking about. I'll be careful, bye."

As soon as Joan hangs the phone up, the music stops. Joan walks back into the living room, and she point to the stereo. "You need to be quiet. I really need to study right now. Unlike you, I still have a life, and I want to make the best out of my life. So shut up."

Joan looks around the room. The Dark Figure is almost on the top of her. The Music starts again. Joan slams her hand down on the stereo. The music stops.

"Hey, that's an expensive piece of equipment," someone says.

Joan screams and spins around. She saw Joey standing in the doorway.

He closes the door. "Why are you beating my things?" he asks.

Joan groans. "Don't tell me you didn't hear that?" She shoots him a curious look.

Joey walks over to Joan. "Hear what?"

Joan sighs loudly. "I mean the music, the loud music. Joey, I think there's a ghost in this house."

"Ah! Ah! Umm, you're having one of those unpredictable days again, huh?" he gives her a dirty look and walks away.

Joan looks at him. "Joey, you know what is strange about the stuff that is going on in this house? You're never around when any of it happens."

"You look beautiful when you're angry." He tries to come close to her.

Joan pushes him away. "This is a serious matter. You shouldn't be joking with it. You don't get it, do you?"

Joey laughs. "What am I supposed to do, huh? You tell me. Would you marry me? Are you listening?"

Joan is speechless. She stares at him like he's a UFO.

Joey smiles and starts to dance around the living room by himself. "Joan, marry me, marry me, marry me!"

"This is the strangest proposal I've ever heard. Marriage is not a piece of candy," Joan responds.

Joey continues to dance around the room by himself. He invites Joan to dance with him every time he's near her. "Joan, I love you, marry me."

"We've shared this house for seven months," Joan says. "You've never said anything about loving me."

"I just did."

Joan laughs uncontrollably. "If this is your best method of proposing to a woman, you suck." Joey goes across the room to give Joan a hug.

The hug has no significance to Joan. To her it's nothing, but a bear hug.

Joey pats Joan on her shoulder. "When you're done with the good doctor, we're going to get a marriage license." He moves closer to kiss her, but she puts her hand on his lips.

Joan can't believe it, she's flabbergasted. "You can't be serious," she looks at him.

Joey rubs his chin. "I've never been more serious."

Joan sees Joey as a very strange man. Her instinct tells her that there's some-thing weird about Joey, but she can't figure out what it is. "Love is supposed to be reciprocated. What if I don't?" Joan asks.

Joey paces around the room, and then he stops and looks at Joan. "My mother told me that love comes with time. I know it will just be a matter of time before you come around."

Joan shakes her head. "That's not what my mother told me," Joan rebuffs.

"So you disagree with my mother?"

"That's right." She paces up and down the room. While validating with her hands, she says, "My mother advised me not to marry a man unless we are compatible. It may be true that love comes with time, but you shouldn't forget that love fades away with time too. People fall out of love. For love to keep going, you and your partner must have common grounds."

"Are you a lawyer?" Joey asks, smiling.

"No, I'm not," Joan replies quickly. "Tell me, Joey. What is it you like about me?"

"You should be a lawyer," Joey says. "You have qualities a man needs in a woman,"

"Huh, like what?" Joan is curious to know.

"Let me finish," Joey says. "If your man gets in trouble, you sure know how to manipulate those lies to save his ass."

"What?" Joan goes ballistic. "Joey, you're not making sense."

"Yes, I am."

"No, you're not," Joan bits her lips. "We're not compatible. First of all, I'll never, ever let my husband do something stupid."

Joey heads for the kitchen. "Joan, don't tell anyone that I proposed to you until after the wedding."

Joan, speechless, watches Joey leave the room.

NINE

The Psychiatrist

Joan is busy dusting the entertainment center in the living room when she hears the doorbell ring. She looks at the time, its 11 AM. "That must be Dr. Ross," she mumbles to herself. She moves sharply to open the door to the office. Dr. Kenneth Ross comes in. The office is businesslike, yet cozy with three large teddy bears sitting on the floor.

"Nice home," Dr. Ross smiles at her.

Joan leaves Dr. Ross and goes to the kitchen to get bottles of water and soft drinks. She maneuvers past Dr. Ross and sits the bottles on the table.

She shakes his hand. "Welcome, Dr."

"Thank you," Dr. Ross responds grimly.

Joan motions for the doctor to have a seat.

"Thanks," says Dr. Ross.

Dr. Ross takes the seat opposite Joan.   He

reaches for his briefcase and pulls out a legal pad and pen. He looks at Joan. "So, how can I help you?"

Joan looks at him, directly. "Before I say anything, I want to make sure this will all be confidential."

"Of course, anything said here today is strictly confidential," he reassures her. "Now tell me what's going on. Are you married?"

Joan shakes her head.

"I'm sorry. I assumed you were, because Pastor Wright told me you were living here with a man. I thought he was your husband."

"No. Joey and I are just roommates, but who knows, anything is possible."

Joan and the doctor stared at each other for a moment.

"Go on, I get paid by the hour."

Joan laughs, and then becomes serious. She leans forward. "I hear stuff and I see things."

Dr. Ross nods and smiles, but Joan does not reciprocate. "Really, it happens all the time."

"I see and hear things around this house all the time; strange things. And my roommate is never around to see any of it. He thinks I'm crazy, but I've never experienced such things until I came to stay here."

Dr. Ross nodded, and starts to scribble on his pad.

"You think I'm crazy too, don't you?" Joan asks.

"Oh, no! Now what is it that you see and hear?"

Joan takes a deep breath. "One morning, I went to take a shower, and the door was locked, and the shower was running." She pauses to take a drink of water. "I waited for like an hour. Finally, I came out of my room and knocked on the door. I thought it was Joey, but as it turned out, he was in his room the whole time. When I opened the bathroom door, the bathroom was empty and there were no signs of the shower being on."

Dr. Ross begins to write again.

Joan continues. "Another time, I went to the kitchen to make coffee, and there was a pot already made. I asked Joey if he made it, and he said no."

Dr. Ross frowns. "And you believe him?"

"Of course," Joan raises her hands. She opens her palms, and then closes them.

Dr. Ross continued to frown, showing signs of disbelief. "The only way it could have happened is if you have a ghost in this house, but I'm pretty sure your roommate made the coffee."

"That's what I thought, too," Joan replied.

"Have you ever considered moving out?" Dr. Ross asked her.

"Oh, I can't do that. I signed a contract for

one year, so if I move I'd still owe for the remaining months," Joan explains. "And I'm afraid he'd take me to court. Moreover, I don't want to ruin my credit."

"That's usually the case. Sometimes it's really difficult to break a lease. Tell him you want to move, and see what he says," he advice her.

Joan takes a deep breath, and then she stares at the ceiling. "I'm afraid he'd say no. He's very inconsiderate."

"If I were you I'd summon the courage to tell him that you intend to move out, and damn the consequences."

Joan gets up and paces around the office. "One day, I heard a voice. It sounded like Joey's voice, but there was something so strange about it. It called my name many times, but it was like an echo," Joan explains. "A minute later, there were footsteps, and they were all around me, on the floor, on the walls, even on the ceiling." She pauses. "Suddenly, I felt something around my neck and I grab my neck. Something was choking me. It was like a large talons wrapped around my neck," Joan turns around to Dr. Ross only to see him fast asleep, his hand barely hanging onto his notepad.

Joan screams, grabs her glass of water, and dumps it on the doctor's head. Dr. Ross jumps up from the chair and shivers. He brushes himself off and soon realizes what happened. Dr. Ross was ashamed. He raised his two hands. "I am so sorry, Joan. I…"

"Close your mouth, it'll be nice if you don't say a word," Joan yelled. "How dare you? Was my story that boring, huh? Was it that boring?"

"Joan, I can explain. We have new twins that have been keeping me up at night. They're just two weeks old."

Joan heads out of the office with Dr. Ross in tow. "I can't believe you. I'm spending hard-earned money on this session, and you're not giving me the service I need."

He follows her, apologizing to her. "Joan, please I'm very sorry."

Joan rushes up the stairs, and walks into her room. Dr. Ross, who has been following her, stops in the hallway. "If you could just hear me out…"

Joan starts to talk to herself as she ransacks the top drawer of her dresser.

Dr. Ross continued to plead from the hallway. "I can understand your being upset with me."

Joan pulls a gun from her dresser and aims it at Dr. Ross. He screams and dives to the floor as she shoots the gun into the air.

Dr. Ross gets up, and starts looking for the

stairs. Joan chases him out of the hallway and fires again.

Dr. Ross stumbles down the stairs, and darts out of the house. Joan goes to the door, fires the last shot, and then slams the door.

After the session, Pastor Wright stops by Joan's house. The two were talking in the living room. Pastor Wright asked Joan about Dr. Ross. "How did it go? He's good, isn't he?"

"No! He's the worst counselor I've ever seen." Joan starts to cry.

Pastor Wright puts her left hand across her shoulder. "What happened? Please tell me."

"I feel like a yahoo after narrating my problems to Dr. Ross."Joan is disappointed in herself. "Pastor Wright, was my story boring?"

"No!" Pastor Wright says. "What is it you are trying to say? Be specific child."

"He slept on me."

The pastor raises an alarm. She couldn't believe it. "Why would he do that?"

"He told me that he has trouble sleeping at night," Joan informs her.

Pastor Wright frowns. "That's silly. What has it to do with you?"

"He tried to justify what he did," Joan groans. "According to him, he had twins two weeks ago. Basically, the wife has been sick, and he's the one taking care of the kids at night."

"If that be the case he should stay home until his wife gets better," Pastor Wright says. "If he continues to fall asleep on his client, he'll lose his clients and his license."

Joan sighs.

Pastor Wright put her right hand on Joan's chin. "Look at me child. I told you this before, and I'm going to say it again. You must trust God and learn how to pray. Prayer holds the solution to every problem."

"I'm trying," Joan mumbles.

"Wipe your tears child. Thank your God that you're okay health-wise."

"Pastor, can I get you something?" Joan asked politely.

"No, Joan. Thank you." Pastor Wright looks around the room to make sure they are alone. She leans in towards Joan. "Joan, the good lord told me that you are about to do something dumb."

Joan asks. "What are you talking about?"

"I was hoping you could tell me what it is."

"Sorry, I've no clue of what you're talking about."

"I'm sure it has something to do with you and your roommate, Joey," the Pastor says. "What's going on between you two? Don't lie to me, I'm psychic."

Joan shakes her head. She takes a deep breath and sits back on her seat. Then she looks at Pastor Wright. "I really don't feel like talking about him right now. I know you two don't care for each other, so I'm really not in the mood to gossip."

The pastor gets annoyed because she's sure Joan is aware of what she's trying to say. "Being in a bad mood has nothing to do with this. You know what I'm talking about. C'mon, spit it out." She tries to persuade Joan to tell her the truth. She goes over to Joan and gets down on one knee in front of her. She gentle pinches Joan on the cheeks and stares into her eyes. "Now you listen to me, don't let that Joey charm you. There's something about him that is very troubling."

Joan stares at the ceiling. "He says the same thing about you. What is it with you two?"

Pastor Wright, angry, picks up her purse and heads to the door and walks out. She's about to walk away when she hears footsteps. She stops and turns around to see Joan walking towards her. She looks into Joan's eyes as Joan approaches her.

"Child, you don't know what you're getting yourself into. Please remain steadfast in prayer." The pastor continues to walk away, and Joan walks back into the house.

TEN

Mr. North & Lori

Mr. North and Lori work for a giant networking company in Brisker, Marry-Cruz. They're both engineers and department managers. Sometime in July, their company sends both of them to Bull Moose for a three-day workshop. It is a hectic seminar with an hour lunch and no breaks. They spend most of their time in the hotel premises, going from their hotel room to the meeting room, and to the hotel restaurant. The last day of the seminar, North and Lori decides to go outside of the hotel for dinner. Since they're new in town, they ask a few people where to find good restaurants. Some of the people they talk to recommend Kinky Square. North suggests they use the bus so they can see a little bit of the city and the people.

The workshop ends at 4 PM, Lori and North catch a bus to Kinky Square. Kinky Square is a beautiful place—it's also known as "Millionaire Square" because it's the area where the rich live in Bull Moose. It's a huge place. They enter into a few stores just to look around, but couldn't buy anything because things are pretty expensive in most of the stores. Finally, they pick a restaurant and dined on grilled salmon, red potatoes and asparagus. They were amazed, how friendly people were in Kinky Square despite their wealth.

"I like this place," North told Lori.

"Well, you and I can't afford to live in this part of the town," Lori says. "It's a rich person's quarter."

"I like to dream big, and think big," North mutters.

"Yeah, it's good to think big, and dream big," Lori replies.

After dinner, they catch the bus back to the hotel. The bus drops them off across the street from the hotel. As they are crossing the street, North's eyes catch a glimpse of a gentleman in a gray suit with blue stripes. He steps backward to take a second look at the gentleman. "Is that really him?"

Lori turns towards North. "Whom are you talking about?"

"I'm talking about him," he says pointing a finger towards the gentleman. "He looks very familiar."

"There are six men there," Lori says, looking at North. "Which one are you referring to?"

"I'm talking about the tall man in gray suit with blue stripes."

Lori turns around to look at the guy.

"Did you see him?" North asks. He's looking towards our direction, now!"

"He looks familiar to me, too," Lori says, as she stretches her neck to better see the man's face. "I'm not sure if it's the person I have in mind, though."

The man turns around and looks at Lori from afar. His nasty look makes her shiver. "North, are you seeing what I'm seeing?"

"Yes, yes, yes," North responds quickly. "He looks exactly the same."

"It could be him," Lori says.

"I think so, too. It must be someone that looks like him."

Lori tries to take another look at the gentleman, but sun won't let her. She shields her eyes from the sun with her right hand, and scurries away from it. When she gets away from the sun, she couldn't see the man anymore. "Where did he go?" she ask Mr. North."

"The group disbanded—and they went their separate ways," North replies.

Suddenly, Lori feels some kind of vibration

from a man that walks past her. She raises her head and looks at him. He wasn't exactly the gentleman she had her eyes on, but he was among the six men she had seen. She runs after him. "Excuse me, sir."

The man stops.

"Sorry to disturb you, sir. My name is Lori," she introduces herself. "And this is my colleague, Mr. North. We're new in town. Do you happen to know Joey Noel? I saw the two of you talking to each other a while ago."

"Why do you ask?" the man asks.

"He's our next door neighbor back home," North explains. "We would like to talk to him."

"I know Joey Noel," the man confirms. "He's my boss at work."

North and Lori both freak out as Lori's heartbeat rises, and Mr. North's head starts to spin.

The man tries to walk away, but Lori stops him. "What's your name?"

The man gets upset. "What do you want from me?" he asks. "My name is Felix."

"Do you have a number where I can reach Mr. Noel?" Lori asks.

Felix pulls up his cellphone, and calls out his work number to Lori. He told her to call the operator and ask for Joey Noel's extension number.

"Thank you, sir," Lori says. "You have a great day."

Mr. North is flabbergasted to hear that Joey actually works. He adjusted his eyeglasses and looks up in the sky. "Lori, did you hear that? Joey has a job."

Mr. North and Lori, both dumbfounded, try to cross the street. Cars are coming from different direction, and drivers are honking at them, but they do not hear anything or pay attention to where they are going. A truck from the left strikes the two of them. They fall on top of each other in the middle of the street. Someone calls the ambulance and they are taken to the hospital. Within a few hours, and after series of x-rays, they were both released with no internal injuries.

When Mr. North and Lori return to their hotel room, they did some research on Joey's company. They are able to find some information on him including his residential address and home phone number. Mr. North suggests they call him.

"It's not necessary," Lori says. "I don't want him to know that we saw him."

"I'm wondering if he sensed that someone was watching him," North asks, softly.

"It's likely," Lori says. "No one will believe we saw him."

"Of course, they won't believe us," North agrees.

"I'll give all the information to his wife," Lori says. "Poor thing, she'll go crazy. She has been raising their three beautiful children by herself."

At 9PM, Lori and North decide to go to the restaurant for a glass of wine. As they are about to enter the restaurant, they see Joey leaving the restaurant through the back door with two men. Lori trembles from head to toe.

Blood runs through Mr. North's veins. The incident brings some closure to the doubts they have been nurturing in their minds. Make no mistake about it; he is the real Joey Noel.

"What in the world is going on?" North asks. "He's been gone for five years. This is not happening."

"How could this be possible?" Lori also asks. "I've never heard of something of this nature in my entire life. This story is bizarre."

Suddenly, Mr. North remembers a story a classmate from college told him some years ago. "According to Dapo, one day he went to the market to buy smoked fish for his mother. Africans have open markets like a 'swap meet.' As he entered the huge Yaba market, he went straight to the aisle where they sold smoked fish. He stopped at a stall, picked up a smoked catfish, and asked the seller for the price. The seller didn't answer, and tried hiding her face from him. She didn't like him, and he wondered why. Then his eyes caught hers, and he immediately recognized her as his dead aunt who passed away a few years ago. Blood ran through his veins and he trembled.

The woman scolded Dapo. "Are you following me," she asked him. "Must you buy the fish from me? Why did you choose my stall?"

Dapo took to his heels. He fainted on his way home. At home he told his parents what happened. They followed him to the market, but she was gone. Her relatives visited her market stall several times, but she never came back to that side of the market again. In most African countries it's believed that the dead frequent their open market to trade.

The day Dapo told him about his dead aunt, he was with Uche. Uche narrated his own story about his uncle, Lazarus, who passed away a year before. Lazarus and his wife, Veronica, were so much in love and inseparable. Even after he died, he continued to visit his wife to have dinner with her. Villagers advised her to leave the house, but she didn't listen to them. According to Uche, his mother, Irene, was on her way to church one evening when she spotted Lazarus in the front of his yard. Chills ran through her.

She scolded him. "I thought you were dead? What are you doing here?"

Lazarus gave Irene a look of confusion, and entered the house.

The next day the news was all over town," Mr. North said.

Lori was frightened at the stories. "I won't sleep tonight," she mutters.

It's the day after the Thanksgiving weekend. Lori's husband, Mr. Buchanan, an editor of a newspaper company has just picked his daughter, Nancy, from the airport. Nancy spent Thanksgiving weekend with her grandmother, Kate. Nancy carries her luggage to her room, and emerges three minutes later with an article she wrote about some kids she had played with at her grandmother's house. She wants her Dad to read the article, and if possible, publish it for her.

Mr. Buchanan adjusts his reading glasses and takes the pages with him to the windows so he could read with better light. He finishes reading about five minutes later, and his eyes are blooming. "These boys have incredible talent," he says, and reaches for his cup of coffee.

Nancy looks at the ceiling, and then her dad. "Dad, do you think it would make a good article?"

Buchanan nods, and hands the article back to Nancy. "Read it and tell me how you think you did."

She reads the article again. "I think I did alright, dad."

Buchanan promises his daughter that he'd take a second look at her article.

"I'll be looking forward to seeing my..."

Lori did not let Nancy finish her sentence. "I have a story that will blow people's mind away," she says.

Her husband and daughter stares at her with their mouths agape.

"What kind of story?" Buchanan asks.

"What's the story all about?" Nancy also asks.

"It's about the walking dead," Lori replies, laughingly, "That remind's, me, I have to call Tasha. I have something to discuss with her."

"The walking dead?" Buchanan laughs.

Tasha Nod, a 32-year-old clerk, is entertaining guests. She's barbequing on a grill in the backyard. She hears the phone ring and walks inside to answer it. "Hello. Yes, this is Tasha Nod." She moves into a more private place.

"I'm sorry, what? What did my husband do? You saw my husband?" Blood runs through her veins. "When and where?"

"This past week," Lori says on the phone.

Tasha slams the plate she's holding on the counter. "Look, I don't know who this is or what kind of game you're playing, but this is really sick. You know that right? This is sickening! Sickening! My husband has been gone for five years! Now you're the fourth person to call me and say this!" Tasha paused. "Do you have an address?"

"Yes, I have his home address and phone number," Lori responds. "I'd advise you to go and check him out."

"Oh, you bet I will." Tasha grabs her handbag, and takes out a piece of paper to write down the information. "What's the address? I'll get to the bottom of this one way or the other."

Tasha hangs up, and throws the phone on top of the plate. She sits down on a chair and starts to cry. A woman standing nearby the grill looks up and sees Tasha. She rushes to her—puts her arm around her shoulder to comfort her.

"What's wrong?" the woman asks.

Tasha looks up and shakes her head. "I miss him, I really do".

The woman has no idea who Tasha is referring to. "Do you want to talk about it?"

"Not really," Tasha replies. "People are not nice. They won't leave me alone."

"If someone is bothering you, tell the person to bit it," the woman advice her.

Tasha, in tears, nods.

The woman tells Tasha to take a break. She help Tasha finish the barbeque.

ELEVEN

The Wedding

Joey and Joan are sitting next to each other on the couch. Joey is busy working on his laptop. They are only three days away from exchanging their vows. Joey dumps his laptop on the couch and starts texting.

Joan turns to Joey. "I know you want to keep the wedding secret, but it would mean so much to me if we could have some family and friends over to celebrate with us after all said and done."

He looks at her. "Baby, the wedding is just three days away. It's too late to send out invitation cards."

Joan summons the courage to face him. "No, it's not. Please would you do it for me?" She shakes her head and bites her lip.

"Sure, I will do it for you, but don't expect any of my family to be here," Joey informs her.

"Why not?" Joan frowns.

"Because they don't live in this state," he explains. "Also, it's too late to invite them. I didn't even mention it to them that I was seeing someone, but towards the end of the year I planned to take a two week vacation to go visit them. It should be sometime in October or November."

"By yourself?" Joan asks.

"No, I'm taking you with me," he replies. "I have to introduce my brand new wife to them."

"Are you sure?" Joan asks, softly.

"Yes."

Joan takes a deep breath, stares at his face, and smiles. Joe smiles back.

"Do you believe me?"

"Yes, I do," Joan lies. "I'll continue to believe everything you tell me until you prove me otherwise."

Joey laughs.

"Why not make the vacation three weeks? That way we can visit my family too," Joan suggest.

"Does that mean you're not going to invite them now?"

"Like you said, it's too late," Joan says. "The wedding is three days away."

Joey shrugs.

Joan walks into the kitchen and takes out a

box of fried chicken from the refrigerator. She places it in the microwave to heat it up. After it's done, Joey walks into the kitchen and Joan hands him a piece.

Joey takes a bite. "Mmm, that's good. Look at all this food. I hope you invited enough people to help eat all this."

Joan did invite some friends and a few of her classmates to celebrate with her, but she did not tell them what the occasion was. Joey did not invite anyone, not even his boss or close associates from work, and that shocked Joan.

"Joey, you did invite your friends, didn't you?" Joan asks.

Joey shakes his head. "No."

"Are you serious? Not even a few co-workers?"

Joey shakes his head again, and Joan throws a wet towel at him. "Are you kidding me? You didn't invite anyone to our reception?"

Joey moves sharply towards Joan to hug her, but she walks away.

"It doesn't matter. What matters is that we'll exchange vows. We'll be husband and wife," he tries to calm her down.

Joan questions his sincerity. "Yes it does matter. Do you really love me?"

He smiles. "Of course I do. You didn't force me to marry you. I asked you, remember?

I'm the one who initiated it. I wanted you," he tries to reassure her. He walks up to her, and kisses her on her cheek.

Joan laughs.

"Now, I do have some news that you may not like," Joey says. "I just got off the phone with my boss and he wants me to come in for a few hours."

Joan becomes angry and pulls away from him. "What? Are you serious? I have friends coming over to celebrate our marriage, and you're bold enough to tell me that you're not going to be here. This is unheard of."

"Honey, it's not like he knew we got married today. No one knows. Your friends don't even know why they're coming over here this evening," Joey counters.

"I can't believe this!" She is pissed.

"Listen, love, I will be back in time to share the good news with everyone and celebrate, I promise." He kisses Joan on her forehead and heads for the door.

At 4 PM, guests start to arrive. Joan opens the door and usher people in. Some guests relaxed in the living room, while others head to the kitchen for food and refreshment.

The last of the guests to arrive is Pastor Wright and her friend, Katz.

"Well, I see you have lots of food," Pastor Wright says, and looks around. "So what's the occasion?"

Joan smiles and hugs the pastor.

"C'mon Joan what's the occasion?" Pastor Wright asks again. "Where's your roommate? Tell him to come down. I promise I won't bite him this time."

The pastor steals the attention, and the room goes silence.

"Joey is not here," Joan informs her. "He'll be back in a few minutes though."

Joan and Thelma begin to bring the food out for the guests.

The phone rings, and Joan answers. "Hello?...Oh, hey baby! What?"

The room goes quiet again.

"Why do you do this to me? It's not fair," Joan yells at him. "Today was supposed to be the happiest day of our lives. Why are you ruining it for me?"

The guests look around uneasily. Pastor Wright gets up from her seat and takes a few steps toward the kitchen so she can hear the conversation clearly.

"Why don't you be honest with your boss? Just tell him we got married this morning, and the guests are expecting you back here at the house... No, Joey, you always do this to me, and end up humiliating me in front of my friends. An hour is too long."

The guests start to whisper to one another.

Joan hangs up the phone and enters the living room with her head down.

"You and your roommate got married?" Edith asks.

Joan nods and tries to hold back the tears. Her friends rally around her, to congratulate and console her.

Pastor Wright stands up, astonished. "Jesus wept! You did what?"

The guests turn to Pastor Wright, and slowly pull away from Joan.

Thelma tries to lighten the mood. "Um, so hey, why didn't you tell us this was a wedding reception? We would have brought gifts. We could have given you a bridal shower."

Pastor Wright went ballistic. "How could you marry a man with such a horrendous dark side? He lied to you, you know that right? He's not with his boss."

Joan frowns. "He's not? Then where do you think he is?" Her face turns red. "I should be going to his office right now." Joan rushes upstairs to grab a coat. When she comes down the stairs, the pastor meets her at the end.

"No, you can't go," the pastor says. "He might not be in his office."

Thelma interferes. "Joan this is stupid. Put the coat down and let's celebrate this wonderful news." Thelma takes Joan's coat and puts it away. She guides Joan back into the living room. A small group surrounds Joan, and continues to congratulate her.

The bride looks at Pastor Wright and swallowed.

"Pastor, please lead us in prayer," Katz requested.

"Yeah, pastor, pray for the newlyweds. Bless their marriage," Edith adds.

Pastor slaps her lap with her right hand. "Hell, no. Plus the groom is not here yet. If he doesn't show up within an hour, this marriage is null and void."

Phillip shouts from across the room. "Hey, I've got some new CD's in my car," he says. "I'll be the DJ for the evening. No charge of course."

A few moments later, the party is in full swing. Philip is standing near the stereo controlling the music, and everyone is dancing. Joan is finally having a good time. No one is paying attention to the time except Pastor Wright who keeps looking at her watch. After two hours of music, the pastor turns the music off. Everyone stops dancing, and all eyes are on her.

"Sit down, you all," Pastor Wright's voice echoes.

The small crowd obeys her.

"Is anyone here related to Joey?" she asks.

"No, we did not invite any of our family members," Joan says. "We're going to visit them sometime in October or November."

"Are you insane? How could you marry a man you know nothing about?" the pastor scolds Joan.

"Okay, Pastor Wright. I'm getting a little bit irritated by you right now!" Joan voices her anger.

"Think for a moment, child! This man never invites friends over, unless it's after midnight. You've never seen any of them, even when it sounds like the house is packed. You try, but the house goes black," Pastor Wright is outraged.

The guests are getting uncomfortable again. Some start to shift in their seats, and some head towards the door.

"You don't think this is strange?" Pastor Wright asks. "How are you going to handle your so-called husband when he decides to show up tonight?" Pastor Wright walks over to the door and opens it. She steps aside and the guest's starts to leave as if there was a silent alarm or command that they could only hear.

When nearly everyone is gone, the pastor gazes at Joan. "What have you done to yourself?

You just stepped into deep troubled water, child."

Joan stares back at the Pastor.

"You've got my number, I suggest you use it," Pastor Wright says. She follows the last person out of the door and slams it behind her. Joan starts to cry.

TWELVE

Joey Returns To the House

Joan enters the kitchen and finds Joey leaning against the counter. She's shocked to see him there, but only for a second. She reaches for a bowl of water and throws it at him.

Joey jumps up, and moves away from her. "Are you out of your mind? We're married now. You should have a little bit more respect for me."

Joan flips. "You know what Joey? You blew it. I'm starting to think it was a mistake marrying you. Where have you been?"

Joey wipes himself with a towel. "I was at the back of the house. I didn't go to my office."

Joan is baffled. "You were at the back of the house doing what? That's unbelievable. You were supposed to be here with me celebrating our union. All my friends were gathered here today, Joey. What's back there that was more important than the celebration of our Marriage?"

Joey shrugged. "I don't know."

Joan stares at Joey, but he avoids making eye contact and continues to dry himself off.

"So you misled me? You lied about your boss?" Joan asks.

Joey nods.

Joan shakes her head and tears begin to flow down her face. She is terribly upset, disturbed, and perturbed. She tries to compose herself, but can't. She slowly and gradually pulls the wedding ring off her finger and lays it on the counter; she then turns to leave the kitchen.

"Hey, stop. What are you doing?" Joey goes after her.

Joan stops, but doesn't bother to look back. "I'll be filing for an annulment tomorrow," she alerts him. She walks out of the kitchen.

Joey runs after Joan and grabs her by her arm. He struggles to turn her towards him. "We need to discuss this."

"There's nothing to discuss, Joey. I'm done. I want this marriage annulled."

Suddenly, Pastor Wright's voice is heard. "That's a smart idea, Joan."

Joan and Joey look up to find Pastor Wright and Katz standing at the front door.

"This guy is not real," Pastor Wright continues.

Joey releases Joan when he sees the Pastor,

and her friend, Katz, and takes a few steps   back. Katz continues to move towards him. She lowers her eyeglasses to the tip of her nose to get a better look at Joey.

Joey looks at Joan. "You see, this is why I left. This woman who calls herself a pastor is nothing but a troublemaker. She irritates me to the bone. You know I can't stand her, yet you invite her anyway."

Joan stares at the ceiling and shakes her head. "I don't care. Her being here in no way justifies what you did."

Katz continues to examine Joey.

"You see what I mean? Tell this woman to quit staring at me," Joey commands. "I don't like people staring at me!"

Because he was annoyed by their presence, Pastor Wright and Katz walked out of the house with no further comment. Joey and Joan stare at each other. Joey's cell phone starts to vibrate in his pocket and then beeps. He pulls it out, looks at it, and then giggles. Joan snatches the phone away from him, and reads the text message.

"What is this?" she asks.

"It's a project I've been working on."

"You actually made this?" Joan is surprised.

"Yep," he replies with pride. "I've been working on this for a long time. The signal goes to a security network, and alerts you anytime someone is coming near your house or property. All I need to do is go to a computer and type in the code number that shows up on the screen, and I can see a video feed of the house or property 24 hours a day."

She hands him the phone. "Wow, that's impressive. And you designed this yourself?"

"Well, my teams and I, but I am the chief engineer as well as the project coordinator," Joey replies.

"I'm very proud of you," Joan says. "Because of this achievement, I forgive you." Joan goes around the corner of the kitchen and picks up her wedding ring. She holds Joey's hand and the two of them heads upstairs.

Joey tries to open the door to his bedroom, but trips over a box full of Joan's things.

"Who left this box here?" Joey asks. When he looks farther down and finds more boxes sitting in the hallway. Joey navigates through the boxes to get into his room. Thirty minutes later, he comes out of his room and heads downstairs.

In the living room, Joan is filing her nails on the couch. Joey comes down the stairs. "Why are all your things scattered upstairs?" he ask her.

"Oh, I was waiting for the opportunity to move my stuff into your room."

Joey frowns and steps back. "Why?"

Joan stops filing her nails and looks up at Joey. "We're married now," Joan exclaims. "I'm your wife, so I should be sharing the same room with you."

"We should have discussed it first," Joey says.

"There's nothing to discuss. We're married now. We're one," Joan replies.

Joey whispers to her. "Well, not really."

Joan gets up from the couch. "And what is that supposed to mean?"

"You see, I'm not like other men," Joey explains. "I'll let you share my room once every six months."

Joan is enraged. She screams, "Why did I get married?"

It hits Joey that "Why did I get married" is the name of a movie. "I watched that movie; both of them. That tells you something right there. There's no marriage without ups and downs."

"Joey, we barely started," Joan starts to cry.

"Crying is not going to do it," Joey says.

Joan pulls out her cell phone and dials a number. "Pastor Wright? Yeah, I really need you right now...Okay, bye." Joan hangs up the phone, and before Joey can say anything, Pastor Wright walks into the house as if she has her own keys. Joan was inside their office at the time.

"I was with a friend right around the corner when you called me." Pastor Wright ignores Joey's presence, and escorts Joan to the couch. "What's the matter, child?"

"I have devastating news. I need your prayers to hang on," Joan informs her. "My husband wouldn't let me move in with him. He said he can only allow me in his bedroom once every six months." She starts to cry again.

Pastor Wright shakes her head. "Lord, have mercy. How long will you cry for this man? So what do you want from God?" she ask Joan. "You want God to change Joey's mind so he could let you into his room more often?"

"Yes," Joan quickly responds.

"This is the strangest prayer request I have ever received," Pastor Wright says. Pastor Wright stands up and spreads her hands to the heavens. "Lord, I am on your legs where you can see me faster, there are too many people in your hands."

Pastor Wright holds Joan's hand, and reaches for Joey's hand so he can join them in prayer, but he walks away.

"In my entire carrier as a pastor, I have always preached unity amongst couples, but this time, I'm praying for division. Joan let's kneel down and pray."

When they finish praying Pastor Wright ask Joan what she's going to do when Pastor Wright leaves.

"I have homework to do," Joan responds.

"You do that, child." Pastor Wright heads towards the door.

THIRTEEN

Joan's Birthday

In the living room, Joey is helping Joan do her homework. Joey looks under the coffee table, and finds three packets of almond cookies. He picks up a packet and shows it to Joan. "Did you buy them?"

"Those cookies?" she asked him. "Aunt Mercy sent them to me for my birthday."

"Oh, yeah, it's tomorrow. Thanks for reminding me," Joey says. He opens the packet, and eats a couple of cookies. "Yummy."

"My aunt is a baker," Joan informs him. "She bakes anything—you name it. I think we might be having some company tomorrow. My friends are coming over with their friends. They are bringing the food, as well."

Joey frowns. "You know I don't like crowds. How many people are coming?"

Joan slides back towards him,   and pinch

him on the cheek. "Oh, I already know that. It's not a lot, at the most fifteen or eighteen people."

"That's a lot," Joey says.

"I didn't get a bridal shower, so they want to make up for it," Joan says. "Please don't tell me you're going somewhere tomorrow."

Joey touches his forehead. "Please don't invite Pastor Wright. If she comes here, I'll leave."

"I hardly ever invite her. She shows up on her own," Joan retorts.

"That lady gets on my dawn nerves. She's creepy."

Joan blinks. "She says all kind of things about you, too."

Joey picks up a bottle of water from the table. He takes off the cap, and drinks from the bottle.

"Joey, that reminds me. Pastor Wright told me that one day, not far from now, I'll find out on my own who you really are." She sees Joey staring at her like she is a total stranger. "Relax; I'm not listening to her."

"I'm going to get some part gears to decorate the house for tomorrow," he changes the subject.

"Well, that's very sweet of you, but I already got some stuff for the decoration," Joan says. "It's in the pantry."

"Great! I'll get started first thing in the morning," Joey walks out of the room. As he ascends the stairway, the Dark Figure returns to the room and hovers behind Joan as she continues to do her homework.

That night, Joan stayed up late to finish her homework. At midnight, Joey marvelously decorated the entire downstairs for her birthday. At 5 AM, he wakes her up, and tricks her to go downstairs with him. He covers her eyes with his hands, and leads her through the dark stairway.

"Joey, I can't see," says Joan.

Joey laughs uncontrollably. "I know that."

"It's not funny, Joey. I'm scared. I'm going to break my neck."

Joey giggles "Aw, come on now, you know I wouldn't let you do that." Joey leads Joan into the living room and then removes his hands from Joan's eyes. Joan is amazed. She's impressed with all the beautiful decorations in every corner of the room. Joan hugs Joey, dearly. "Oh my God, it's so beautiful. I didn't know you were this creative. Wow!"

"Hey, I must recall, you're the one who bought all the stuff," Joey reminds her. "I just placed them in the right spot."

"Man, you did a wonderful job. What about the cake?" Joan asks.

He has a devilish grin on his face. "The cake is somewhere in this room."

Joan smiles. "Where is it? I don't see it."

Joey giggles. "Silly you, it's right on the coffee table in front of you."

Joan looks around, and sure enough, there is a large birthday cake sitting on the table. "How did it get there? It wasn't there before."

"It was there, but you were too excited that you didn't notice."

"Can I have a piece?"

"Hey, you have to wait until all your friends gets here," he whispers.

At 3 PM, the living room is bubbling with soft chats and laughter, and the party is getting started. Joan is busy talking with a group of girls and Joey is busy with the stereo. Joan, Edith, Alice, and Bianca walk into the kitchen, and Phillip and his friends Maurice and Anita followed them.

"Wow, who decorated the house?" Anita asked. "This is very creative."

"Actually, it was Joey," Joan replies.

The name "Joey" catches the attention of Joan's girlfriends and some of them laughed.

"I wish my husband was that creative," says Anita.

Alice gives Anita a nasty look.

Joan turns around and looks at Anita. "Are you married?"

"No, but I'm engaged."

Diana changes the subject. "I think I'm having a hard time completing my science project in Dr. Rex's class."

"Forget that class, I'm dropping it on Monday?" Thelma informs them.

Philip can't believe what he just heard. "Thelma, how can you drop the class? This is your last semester in school, and you need this class to graduate," he says.

Thelma waves Phillip off. "I'm going to take it in the summer. Some friends told me that it's easier if you take it with Dr. Oronzo in the summer."

Phillip stares at Thelma. "Don't believe everything you hear. They might be feeding you wrong information."

"I'm considering dropping the class, too. It's too hard for me," Diana says. "I'm glad it's not a requirement for my degree program."

Joey gets irritated with the conversation. This is not what he wants to hear, and as a result, he pokes his head around the corner. "Ladies and gentlemen, it's time to eat."

"I agree. It's time to eat," Philip laughs aloud.

Joan smiles.

"Joey, it seems like you're starving," Joan says, and smiles at him.

"I haven't eating all day," Joey responds. "I was waiting for your friends to bring the food."

Downstairs is full of people eating and socializing—Joan and Joey are sitting on the couch. Edith is busy carrying a tray of food around the room. She asks Phillip if he needs anything.

"No thanks. I had enough food already," Philip responds.

"What about you, Anita?" Edith asks.

"No thanks. I'm trying to shed some pounds," Anita replies, arrogantly.

"Okay guys, let's get those fabulous presents out of their box," Angela suggests. She picks up one of the presents and looks at it. "I'll open them." She opens the gift without Joan's approval. Joey gives her a dirty look.

"This first one is from Diana," Angela says.

"What is in it?" Joan asks.

Angela opens the gift. "They are frosted drinking glasses."

Joan smiles faintly and takes the gift from Angela. "They are lovely. Thank you, Diana."

Angela picks up a blue envelope from the

floor. She opens it. "It's a gift certificate for a hundred dollars. It's from Philip."

"Thanks, Phillip," Joan says. "I'm going shopping tomorrow."

"I think you deserve more from me. You've been my best friend for the past ten years," Phillip says with a grin. "It's only a small token."

"Wow! Ten years," Joey mutters. "I can only keep a friend for six months."

"Really?" Phillip asks.

Joan pats him on his leg. "Come on, Joey, that's not true at all."

The next gift is from Thelma.

"Thelma, where did you get these books? I've been looking for them for three months." Joan is happy about the gift.

"I found them at a bookstore on my side of the town. The store has lots of great stuff."

"Thank you so much," Joan says.

Suddenly, Anita starts to cough uncontrollably. and every one turns their attention on her.

"Anita, what's wrong," Phillip asks.

"I smell something funky?"

"Something like what?" Joan asks curiously. "I can't smell anything myself."

"I do smell something," Diana backs Anita's claim. "It smells like a dead animal or something."

"You mean there's a dead animal in this room?" Edith gets up and starts sniffing the air. The smell leads her to Joey. She bends over and sniffs his shoulder.

Joey jumps off the couch. "Hey, what the hell are you doing?" He walks to the trash, dumps his plate in it, and then leaves the room. As he leaves he thanked everyone for coming over. "I have some work to do." He rushes for the stairs, and at the end of the stairway he turns around and gives Diana and Anita a dirty look.

"Wow, he really stunk. What kind of cologne does he wear?" Edith asks.

"You mean Joey was the one smelling like that?" Emily stares at the ceiling.

Anita and Diana ignored Emily's question. "He gave us a dirty look in the stairway. Did you see that?" Anita whispers to Diana.

"Yes, and his eyes were glittery like the eyes of a witch," Diana responds.

"I saw that, too," Anita confirms. "I noticed something else."

"What?" Diana's eyes turn red.

"His legs were kind of floating in the air. They weren't touching the floor."

"Would you all stop it?" Phillip yells at them.

Joan stands up—walks towards the front door, and opens the door. "Thanks for coming.

This party is over. I'll open the rest of the gifts later."

"But Joan…" Thelma didn't finish her sentence.

Joan starts to cry. "Thank you for coming. Please leave!"

The group slowly gets up and files out. Joan closes the door, and turns around to find Joey sitting on the couch as if he never left the room. She walks straight to him, and gives him a hug. "I'm sorry, Joey. You shouldn't be insulted in your own house. That's terrible. I don't even know what they were talking about."

"You handled it like a true wife. I thank you." Joey is grateful, and he kisses her on her cheek.

"I'll never let any woman insult you," she whispers.

Joey smiles at her. "Thanks."

FOURTEEN

Inside The Girl's Bedroom

It's a dark raining night with thunderstorms. Anita wakes up at the middle of the night, and looks around her room. She notices something move. She hears loud voices coming from the dark, laughing at large, and footsteps following after that. They get louder and louder. "Diana," she whispers to her roommate.

Diana continues to snore.

Anita shakes her gently. "Diana," she says. "Are you awake?"

Diana sits up. "What?"

"Are you awake?" Anita asks again.

Diana doses off and goes back to sleep.

Anita rolls to her left and turns on the light switch. The light increases the laughter tremendously.

The footsteps are heard in every corner of the room. Boom! Boom! Boom!

Anita panics. She looks around, but can't see anyone.

Diana moves her legs around, but did not wake up.

There's a tall figure dressed in black robe walking around the room laughing. He sees her, but she can't see him.

Anita shakes Diana again, gently. "Wake up, Diana."

Diana turns around. "I'm awake. Why did you wake me up?"

The light turns itself off.

Anita pointed into the dark. "Something is out there," she says.

Thunder crashes into the room.

Anita screams. "I know you are in there. Come out. What do you want from us? Please go away. I don't remember doing anything wrong to anyone."

Diana jumps up from her bed. "What's wrong with you, Anita?"

Anita jumps up from her bed, as well.

The laugher and footsteps quiet down.

"There's a shadow walking all over the room," Anita says.

"Where's the shadow?" Diana asks, fearfully. "I can't see it."

The footsteps and the laughter come back again.

"I want you to listen carefully, the footsteps are all over the room," Anita informs Diana. "The laughter is getting louder and louder. I'm going deaf."

"I heard a sound around the window. What is that?" Diana whispers.

"That's what I've been trying to tell you all along. There's something in the room," Anita says. "I can't see it, but it's right in here."

The bedroom door flies open.

Anita opens her mouth. "Huum!"

The girls head to the door, but it closes before they can get out. They try to open the door, but it wouldn't open.

Finally, the door flies open, and the girls run out of the house. They end up taking shelter somewhere else.

"I hope whatever it is doesn't follow us down here," Anita says.

Five days later, Edith comes to visit Joan in her house. They were both sitting in the dining room drinking coffee. Edith looks around the room. "Is your husband here?" she asks Joan.

Joan frowns. "No, why do you ask?"

"There's a rumor around," Edith informs her.

"About what?" Joan frowns.

Edith stares at Joan directly on her face.

"Anita and Diana's apartment might be haunted."

"Are they sharing the same apartment?" Joan asks, surprisingly. She didn't even know they live together.

"Yes, they're roommates. They fled the apartment because things were moving around in their room. It was pretty bad, I guess. They're losing some friends because they think they're on drugs or sick in the head."

Joan bursts into laughter.

"Rumor number 2 is that it started right around the time of your birthday."

"Tell those two bitches to shut their mouths and go to blazes. If I hear them mention my husband's name one more time I will..." Joan was furious.

"Joan, this is serious. They went to see Pastor Wright about it. They're really scared," Edith explains.

"There's nothing wrong with my husband."

Edith is shocked. She doesn't know what to say.

"You are not married, Edith. Wait until you get married, and then you'll know how it hurts when friends make a fool of your husband," Joan feels like kicking her out of her house.

"Joan, they said they saw a shadow, a figure of some kind. It wore a black robe."

"I'm sick and tired of this, Edith. I think you should go," she tells her.

As soon as Edith leaves her house, Joan goes into the kitchen to make fruit salad. She's cutting the strawberries when Joey comes in and wraps his arms around her from behind.

"What do you want? I'm cutting your favorite fruit, strawberries."

"Good. I am lucky to have someone who takes such good care of me," Joey says. "Which one of your friends was it today?"

Joan turns around and looks at him. "How do you know I had company, today?"

"I dreamt it," he says and frowns. "You don't believe me?" Joey steals some strawberries from the cutting board.

"There's a rumor, I guess about us."

"Okay." Joey looks angry.

"Anita and Diana's apartment is haunted, and they say things started around my birthday. Remember they smelled weird cologne in here."

"What did you tell them?" Joey asks.

"I haven't talked to any of them directly," Joan replies. "But when I do, there'll be a price to pay. Everyone blames us for their problems."

Joey smiles at her. "That's my girl."

Four days later, Emily, Anita, Edith and Diana pay Joan a surprise visit. They were all sitting together in the living room. The tension can be sensed.

"Let's talk about the rumor. You are carrying rumors that your house is haunted because you attended my birthday?" Joan mutters. "Would you please explain to me how you're able to connect the two? How did you do the math?"

"I never said that," Anita says with a grin.

"I don't care what the two of you think or say, as long as you leave me, my husband and our lovely home out of it," Joan warns them. "Got it?"

"Hey, wait a second. I didn't tell anyone about Joey," Diana denies.

Emily is silent. Something has caught her attention at the front door. The other girls become troubled by her silence and disconnection.

"What's going on?" Joan asks Emily. "Are you still here?"

"Anita, did you see that?" Emily asks.

"Yes, I saw someone in a black robe come in through the door," Anita replies.

Edith panics.

"How come you saw someone come through the door when the door is not open?" Joan asks Emily. "Besides, we have an alarm."

"Are you seeing another Halloween ghost? Please keep whatever you see to yourself, I don't want to be a part of it," Edith warns the girls.

"It looks exactly like the one I saw in our bedroom a few days ago," Anita says.

"Emily, you and Anita are not making any sense," Edith condemns their behavior.

"How come no one believes me?" Emily frowns.

"I didn't see the robed figure in our house. Anita did," Diana says. "She said he was walking around our bedroom with a gun."

Joan did not see anything, so she just sat and listened. She had the feeling that the girls are going insane, and finally says something. "It seems like you are going crazy. I am not seeing anything."

"Diana, if you didn't see the ghost yourself, how do you know you were haunted?" Edith asks.

"There were footsteps and laughter in the room, kitchen and bathroom," Diana says. "I heard those ones."

Emily continues to look towards the front door.

"I think the two of you were hallucinating," Joan says.

"We're not hallucinating, Joan," Anita defended herself. "He's really here. I can feel the ENERGY?"

Edith looks at Anita, weirdly.

Joan got angry. "No one else is feeling this ENERGY, but you. It's my house."

Something is going on, but Joan is not feeling it. "I can't see anything," Joan says.

"Anita, did you tell anyone other than those of us here about your experience?" Edith asks.

"I hear footsteps. I think I have heard those footsteps before," Joan confirms.

The girls focus their attention on Joan.

"Please tell us," Emily says. "Where did you hear it the first time?"

The footsteps double and Joan freaks out. "Joey? Joey, is that you?"

Emily, Edith, Diana, Anita are dumbfounded. They are amazed that Joan knew something about the footsteps. Since Joey doesn't respond or show up, Joan instructs the girls to close their eyes and pray. After they open their eyes they find Joey, Pastor Wright and Katz standing above them.

"What is going on here?" Pastor Wright asked the girls.

"I am glad you are home," Joan runs to take shelter in her husband's arms. "You won't believe what happened here today."

Pastor Wright gazes at Joey.

"You again," Joey says.

"I'm disappointed in you. I thought we put this part of you behind us, Joey," the Pastor says.

112

"You know what? You are not welcomed here, lady," Joey warns, Pastor Wright.

Pastor Wright glares at Joey. "You are very clever, aren't you? Oh yes, you know how to deceive people. Why are you doing this to these poor girls?"

Joey explodes. "What the hell are you talking about? You are the one that hovers about, and enter homes without permission. I think you're evil, Mable."

Pastor Wright moves closer to Joey. "I beg your pardon? Lord, have mercy! The pot is calling the kettle black, eh?"

Joey moves backwards. "I'm warning you, Pastor! Stay away from me!"

Pastor Wright and Katz laughed uncontrollably. The girls are confused about the feud.

"What is going on with you two?" Joan asks. "How long have you known each other?"

"Never," Joey replies.

"I'll fast and pray that God opens your wife's eyes. I will pray it happens soon," Pastor Wright says.

"Now, get out of my house," Joey commands.

Pastor Wright and Katz leave the house reluctantly, and Joey is relieved to see them leave.

FIFTEEN

The Living Room

Joan comes down the stairs to see Joey sulking on the sofa crying.

She rushes to console and embrace him. "Honey, what's the matter? Tell me, I'm your wife."

"I am afraid of losing you. I don't want to lose you," Joey tells her.

Joan nods.

"I love you, but I'm afraid that evil pastor friend of yours will tear us apart," he says.

"Don't worry, I will tell her to stay away from you."

The following day, Joan is busy doing her homework in the living room when her phone starts to ring. She picks it up, and it's Pastor Wright.

"Pastor Wright, I'm glad you called. I plan

on calling you sometime today. Joey has been crying. He's afraid you might ruin our marriage. Please don't do that," Joan pleads. "We love each other. Now tell me the truth, did you know my husband before I moved in with him? It seems like it, no? Why do you hate each other so much?"

"If you want answers about Joey's past maybe you should take a look around his room. He does let you in his room once in a while, doesn't he?"

Joan pauses and then sighs. "Yes, he does once in a while. I'll try to do what you said."

"It's not going to be easy?" Pastor Wright says. "He's going to get you, but do it anyway. You might find some clues."

Joan, after talking to pastor Wright decides to go into Joey's room to see what she can find. While in front of his bedroom door, she loses the courage and momentum to open his door and becomes frightened. When she eventually gives in and opens the door. She ransacks the room and searches his bed, drawers, bookshelves, and closet. After she finishes, she quickly tries to put things back where she found them. She turns around, to see Joey standing in front of her.

Joan screams. "Honey, you scared me!"

Joey is enraged. "What are you doing in my room?"

"I lost my ring," Joan lied. "I've been looking for it everywhere."

"You're looking for your ring in my room?" Joey's face turns red. "You have never been in my room, Joan. Ever!"

Joan's heart starts to pound. "I thought you were at work? How did you . . .

Pastor Wright appears behind Joey with Katz besides her.

"That is a good question," Pastor Wright says. "How did you get here, Joey?"

Joey became irritated. "You again?"

"Were you here all along, Joey? We have been downstairs this whole time and we didn't see you come in?" Katz asks.

"You must have closed your eyes, and did not pay any attention," Joey mutters. "Pastor Wright, I thought I warned you to stay away from me," he adds.

"How long are you going to play this game?" Pastor Wright asks him.

"What game? What are you talking about," Joey asks and looks at the pastor strangely.

"Don't act as if you don't know what I am talking about," Pastor Wright says.

"Get out! You are a destroyer! You are destroying my life!"

"How can I destroy your life, Joey? You don't have a life," Pastor Wright fires back.

Joey is troubled. He seems very much concerned and on the edge of breaking down.

"You heard me, Joey. Do you have anything to say to me?" Pastor Wright asks him.

Joey storms downstairs and leaves the house, slamming the door. Katz observes him through the bedroom window as he peels out in his car.

Joan leaves Joey's room and goes to the den to talk to Pastor Wright. "There's nothing in his room, nothing out of the ordinary."

"Perhaps, Joan. But what other clues are you looking for? He has already shown you who he is?" Pastor Wright tells her.

"How?" Joan wonders. "I want you to be specific."

"C'mon, Joan. You are not that dumb," says Pastor Wright.

Suddenly, the pastor's eyes begin to follow some movement. She turns in a circle and her eyes move up and down the walls and along the ceiling. She then stares directly at Joan. "Your husband is a devil's workshop. May the lord have mercy on him?" Pastor Wright says, and heads to the door with her friend Katz.

Joan goes into the kitchen for a glass of water. After her first drink, she spies her troubled husband pacing up and down the living room floor. He doesn't seem to notice her, so she waits and watches. "What are you doing, Joey?"

Joey shivers and his face is covered in tears. Joan rushes to him and guides him to a chair in the kitchen.

"What's wrong," she asks. "I have never seen you like this before."

"I don't feel good. It's like my body is trying to tell me something," Joey whispers to his wife.

"Do you want to see a doctor?"

"There's nothing a doctor can do for me. I have some personal issues to resolve."

Joan sits next to him and holds his hands.

"Is it too personal that you cannot tell your wife? That's messed up. Let me make you a cold drink. Maybe that will calm you down."

"A Cold drink won't do it either. I am going to my room to lie down." Joey gets up and goes upstairs.

Later that day, Joan is doing her homework in the living room. Joey comes back downstairs and stands on one foot with a big brown bag slung over his shoulder.

"I finally submitted my new invention to my director," he informs Joan.

"What did he say?" Joan asks.

"He said he is going to review it with another director before noon. Hopefully, they do it today, so he can present it at the board meeting tomorrow."

"You seem pretty excited," Joan tells him, smiling.

"Of course I am excited. If it's approved by the board, that invention will yield millions in its first year."

"I am proud of you."

"I am going to my room to do some work." Joey leaves the living room.

Joan continues to do her homework. The door bell rings, but she ignores it. It continues to ring, and she continues to ignore it. She goes upstairs, uses the bathroom and returns to the living room. She peeps through the hole on the door, and sees no one there. Well, it must be someone trying to sell us something, she thinks. She returns to the sofa and doses off.

SIXTEEN

Tasha's Visit

Joan is sleeping on the couch, when the doorbell rings again. Frustrated, she gets up and walks to the front door and looks through the peep hole. She sees a woman. "Uh, this face looks familiar," she mumbles to herself. She looks at the entry table in the foyer where there's a picture of Joey and his ex-wife. It's the same woman.

She opens the door. "Hi, I'm Joan. Can I help you?"

Tasha smiles at Joan. "Yes, um, let me make sure I am in the right place. Is this 2312 Figueroa Avenue?" Tasha asks.

"Yes, it is. Are you looking for someone?"

Tasha pauses. It was hard for her to mention her husband's name. "Yes, I'm looking for my husband, Joey Noel. Is he here?"

"Yes, he is. You may come in?"

Tasha enters the house, and sees the family

picture on the wall. She shudders. Joan is troubled by her reaction. "Is everything alright" Joan asks.

"Yes, yes. I was just looking at the picture. It reminds me of something," Tasha said with a soft voice.

"Have a seat," Joan welcomes her. She gathers her books and assignments from the table, and puts them away. She turns on the television, and calls upstairs for Joey. "Joey? You have a visitor!"

Joan sits next to Tasha on the sofa. "I can't believe it! I finally get to meet you. Joey speaks so highly of you and the children. When was the last time you saw my husband? Oh, sorry...I mean your husband."

Tasha smiles faintly. "It's been a while."

Joan is curious and nervous. "You have three children together, right? Does Joey support them? He talks about you and the kids all the time, but I'm not sure whether or not he supports them financially."

This question makes Tasha uncomfortable. Joan notices tears coming from Tasha. "I'm sorry about the questions. I didn't mean to hurt you."

Joan felt sorry for bombarding her with questions. "Can I get you something to drink?"

"Water will be fine," Tasha responds.

Joan offers Tasha a tissue. She walks into the kitchen for a glass of water. She comes back

121

and gives Tasha a bottle of water, and then continues to ask questions.

"Sorry to bug you, Tasha, but I'm curious," Joan says. "Joey acts weird sometimes. Did he ever act that way when you were living together?"

"What do you mean he acts weird? Be specific."

Joan is shaken. She looks at the stairs. She thinks she saw Joey coming downstairs. "Don't worry about it, Joey. C'mon down! You have a surprise visitor. It's about time someone visits you."

"No one visits him?" Tasha asks in disbelief.

"Yes, no one visits him. We have lived here for a year now and you are the first person to visit him in the daytime."

Tasha opens her bottle of water and drinks a little bit. Being at the house troubles her. "Did he tell you why he doesn't want visitors? His parents and siblings would like to visit."

"He doesn't like people visiting him," Joan responds.

"Doesn't he have friends?" Tasha asks.

"He says he does, but I have never met them. They only visit him at midnight."

"Why at midnight?" Tasha is suddenly distracted. She's stunned by the sight of someone in robe coming down the stairs carrying big bags.

"Did you see that?" Tasha asks Joan.

"See what?" Joan asks.

"I just… I just saw a robed figure come down the stairs with bags."

Joan is not interesting in what Tasha is telling her. "Tasha, how long were you two married before getting a divorce?"

"We were never divorced. I'm still married to him," Tasha replies.

Joan goes ballistic. "Joey, you need to come down here and explain yourself! I can't believe you are a bigamist. How can you be married to two women at the same time? You lied about being divorced."

Joan races upstairs and kicks on Joey's door. The door flips open, but Joey was gone, with all his belongings. What he left in the room were 24 burning candles of all colors, and a note about all the money he has in the bank. "Joey, what in the world is going on here? Where are you hiding? Your wife is downstairs waiting for you. You have a lot of explaining to do! Please come out!"

Joan went crazy. "Joey! Joey! Joey! Joey, come out! How can you disappear in this house?" She moves from room to room and continues to call out his name. The last room she checked was the bathroom.

Joan calls from upstairs. "Tasha, I can't find Joey."

Joan continues to look for Joey. "Joey! Joey! How can you disappear from the house?" Joan couldn't believe it. "We have only one entrance in this house."

Joan returns to Joey's room to investigate the candles. She wonders where and how he got the beautiful candles. Did he know his wife was coming before he bought the candles? Then it hit her that Joey actually hated candles. He once warned her never to bring candles into the house. If he really hated candles, why did he buy them? Was he lying to her? There were so many unanswered questions.

Joan runs downstairs. "Tasha, Joey is gone. I can't find him."

Tasha opens her eyes wide. "What do you mean he's gone?"

Joan leads Tasha upstairs. Tasha is terrified.

"Are you sure he's not hiding somewhere in the house?" Tasha asks her.

"No, I looked everywhere for him. Look for yourself."

Tasha looks around the room. "This is serious. How many outlets do you have in this house?"

"Only the one downstairs," Joan responds.

"How did he get out of the building?" Tasha wonders how it could be possible. "Could he be the shadow that I saw walking out of the front door—carrying bags in his hands?"

Joan stops and thinks. Her eyes glaze over.

"Joan," Tasha calls. "Are you listening to me?"

"Yes, I'm trying to remember something."

"I couldn't have come here if I had known he has another wife," Tasha says. "Now he has gone back to heaven."

Joan and Tasha stare at each other, and Tasha begins to cry.

"Tasha, you are not making any sense. What do you mean by he's back in heaven?"

Tasha holds Joan's arms. "Let's go downstairs, and I will tell you who my husband really is."

Downstairs, the women sit together at the dining room. Tasha stares at the ceiling and tears of pain roll down her face.

"This is difficult for me, but I must tell you the truth. Over the past year, four people have called me to tell me that they have seen my husband in the city of Bull Moose. I didn't believe them," Tasha informs her. "I thought they were crazy. The last person to call me gave me this address, and that is why I am here—to see him myself. Unfortunately, he didn't have the guts to face me. The kids miss him so much. He was a perfect husband and father."

"I still don't get it. You're beginning to sound like Pastor Wright," Joan's eyes widen.

Tasha rises from her seat and starts pacing the room. "What I am trying to tell you is that— Joey was an engineer."

"I know that he is an engineer," Joan says. "He recently invented something that is worth millions of dollars, it might even be billions."

Tasha moves away from Joan and continues her story. "One night Joey and two of his friends were coming home from a party around 3AM, and they saw a fire in a two story house. They stopped to see if they could help the people who were trapped in the burning building. They saved the owner of the house, but Joey......" she pauses and then continues. "I remembered the phone call from the police, it was awful. Since then, I have missed him every single day."

"How long ago was this?" Joan asks.

"Five years ago," Tasha replies.

Joan's body starts to tremble. "This explains all the strange things that have been going on in the house. The house has been haunted for quite a while, and none of the events happen when Joey is here. But since we got married I haven't been seeing those strange things anymore. He used to call me crazy lady. I didn't know he was the one doing all those things to me."

Joan runs around the whole house like a mad woman, screaming. "I can't believe this. I have been living with a ghost!"

"I know you love him," says Tasha.

Joan stops yelling and looks at Tasha. "Yes, I love him with all my heart."

Joan's friends, after hearing the story, come to the house and rally around her. Everyone is solemn but hopeful. Tasha is among them.

After being consoled for some time, Joan changes from being heartbroken to anger.

"Tasha, you made a mistake coming here," Joan screams at her. "Your stupid visit has cost me my husband. If you knew he was dead five years ago, why did you come looking for a dead man?"

Tasha is shocked and saddened.

"People were calling to tell me they saw him. I didn't believe them because I knew he had been dead for five years. It was a mystery. I hadn't a clue that this could happen. It's like a dream."

Everyone there was confused, but sympathized with the victims, Tasha and Joan.

"What is going on?" Pastor Wright asks.

"This is Tasha. She's Joey's first wife and the mother of his three children," Joan says.

"He has another wife?" Diana is surprised.

"Pastor, I owe you an apology. Anita and Diana, I apologize," Joan was somber.

"Did you all know that Joey is…a living ghost?" Joan asks.

"The Living Ghost," Pastor Wright nods. "Yes, I did. Do you remember the day I told him that I wouldn't want to see him in my church, because there we do not look for the dead among the living! He haunted you for a while, Diana and Anita. I tried to tell you, but you didn't understand. Where is he now?"

"He vanished with all of his belongings as soon as his wife entered the house," Joan informs the pastor and her friends. "All that was left in his room were 24 burning candles of different colors and a note."

"Did he see her face to face?" pastor Mable Wright asks.

"No, he didn't have the guts," Joan replies.

Everyone in that room is shocked by the story.

"What did the note say?" Pastor Wright asks.

"It contains a piece of information about his bank account, and the shares he has on the product he invented," Joan says.

"This sounds like an African story. Pastor Wright, you should have told Joan the truth," Diana says.

"She wouldn't have believed me. This young generation doesn't listen to anyone, so you learn the hard way," Pastor Wright bites her lip.

"Diana, what do you mean by it sounds like African story?" Katz asks.

"My parents hosted foreign students for thirteen years. I mingled with all of them, and those from Africa used to tell me bizarre ghost stories."

All eyes were on Diana. They want to hear some of the ghost stories.

"Justice, a 22-year-old physics student from Africa told me a story about his uncle, Mike. Mike and his wife had seven children. Mike made a lot of money working for the city. After he turned sixty, he became really sick and stopped working. When money stopped coming in, his wife deserted him, and moved to the city with their children. He was alone in the village, and died a lonely man. When his wife and kids heard about his death, they returned to the village for his burial. Two days after he was buried, the wife was coming out of her room around 7AM, and she saw him sitting in his rocking chair in the living room, rocking himself up like he used to do. His wife screamed, and the whole family gathered to see what was happening. It was like a movie. Every morning, he'd come out at 7AM, and stayed in his chair 'til noon,' and then disappeared. He did that for two weeks; as a result, the whole family fled in fear and never came back."

Diana continued. "Terry, a 30-year-old medical student once told me a story about a pretty girl named, Comfort. Comfort used to work in a restaurant and bar. She gave the best service, and customers loved her. She made a lot of tips because she was nice and friendly. One day her ride didn't show up, and she begged a coworker to give her a ride home. On their way to her home, the man asked her where she lived exactly. Although she lived there for three years, she didn't know the name of the street or the number of the house. The man thought that was odd. He let her describe the place, and her description matched a lonely area of the city where no one lived, but the dead. The man became frightened, and tried to persuade her to spend the night at his house. "I'll take you home on my way to work in the morning," he said. Comfort refused. She wanted to go home that night. They argued back and forth, but eventually, the man took her to his house against her will. Inside his house, he took off his clothes, and entered the bathroom to take a shower. By the time he came out, Comfort had vanished, and what he found in his living room will surprise you."

"What?" Emily asks.

"He saw three big coffins in his living room. She was a ghost," Diana trembles.

They were all shocked.

"There's another one," Diana says. "An English boy told me this one. I can't remember his name. According to him there was a huge church in the city where his parents used to live many years ago. A man called Thomas was unanimously chosen by the church to ring the eighty pounds church bell every Sunday morning, at 9AM, and 11AM. When Thomas passed away at 77, the church appointed Francis to replace Thomas. The first day Francis came to ring the bell, he saw Thomas already ringing the church bell."

"Wow," they were flabbergasted.

"Then what happened?" Pastor Wright looked at Diana straight in the eyes.

Diana continued. "Francis went home. He showed up again at 11AM, and Thomas was still their ringing the bell. He ran into the church and reported the incident to the priests. No one believed Francis.

"How could that be?" they asked.

"Thomas continued to ring the bell every

131

Sunday morning. Finally, the church performed a ritual to get rid of him."

"The presence of ghost is more visible and lively in some countries and ethnicity than others," Pastor Wright says grimly.

"Pastor Wright, is he still here?" Joan asks. "I want to say something to him. I love him."

Pastor Wright pulls Joan closer to her. "Listen, child, we should be celebrating. He's out of this house and off the earth—maybe forever," says the pastor.

Joan runs around the house, screaming. "I can't believe this. I lived with a ghost, and we slept in the same house every day for months."

"What was he like?" the women became inquisitive.

"Damn nonsense, bitches!" Joan yelled, and then her expression changed.

"What's the matter?" Tasha asks.

"Something just hit," Joan says.

"What?" Pastor moves closer to her.

"About six months ago, Joey's company had a huge party that about 400 people attended. They invited executives from other branches of the company from all over the states," Joan says. "Even their competitors were invited. Joey was supposed to receive a leadership award that day. We were supposed to go together in his car, but at the last minute he changed his mind. He told me to drive myself because he might stop somewhere to pick up something for the party. I accepted. At the party Joey was nowhere to be found. I was by myself. I roamed around the whole building in shame looking for my husband. Ten minutes before the awards were presented; he sent me a text message to accept the award on his behalf. I was perturbed. It was one of the worst days of my life. I drove straight home after receiving the award. I didn't want to wait till the end of the party. As I opened the door, Joey was sitting in the living room reading the newspaper."

"Did he tell you why he ditched you?" Tasha asks.

"Yes," Joan replies. "He didn't want to run into familiar faces."

"There you go, that explains everything," Pastor Wright cracks up.

SEVENTEEN

The Board Meeting

Joey was scheduled to attend his company's corporate executive meeting at 2 PM, on the day he disappeared. At 2 PM, everyone shows up except Joey. He had never been late in a meeting before. They waited until 3:30 PM, but still no signs of him, or a phone call.

Dr. Greg, the president of the company, asks Mr. Monster, Joey's direct boss, if he had talked to Joey that day.

"No," Mr. Monster responds, quickly.

"When was the last time you talked to him," Mr. Dobson asks.

"Joey called me last night, and we talked briefly about today's meeting," Mr. Monster says.

Mr. Dobson volunteers to call Joey's cell. The phone beeped but did not ring.

"I've his home telephone number," Mr. Monster says.

Dobson tries his house number. Pastor Wright answers the phone. "Is Joey there?" Dobson asks.

"May I know who is calling, please," Pastor Wright asks.

"This is Mr. Monster. I'm Joey's immediate boss at work."

Pastor Wright busts into laughter. "You're looking for Joey?"

"Yes, he didn't show up for meeting at 2 PM. We're still waiting for him."

"I'm really sorry, Monster. Joey has gone back to heaven. That's where he belongs," Pastor Wright says. "He was here, temporarily."

Mr. Monster frowns. He didn't get it, just like everyone else.

Joan came to the phone and explains to him what happened. Mr. Monster calls the office right away, and the whole company is in disarray. People that worked with Joey tell different stories about their strange encounters with him.

Angie tells a story about how she walked into Joey's office looking for him, but he wasn't there. As she was coming out, Joey was right behind her. "Were you looking for me?" he asked her. "Yes, but you were not there?" Angie replied. Joey asked Angie if she was blind—because he was sitting in his executive chair doing his work inside the office, at the time."

Mr. Comrade recounts his own encounter with Joey the day the two of them went to lunch. Joey excused himself to use the bathroom, and never came back. Mr. Comrade having waited for more than thirty minutes, decided to eat without Joey. When he was about to leave, Joey showed up from nowhere praising the restaurant for the good food. Mr. Comrade was speechless. He asked Joey where he was, and Joey claimed he was sitting next to him enjoying his lunch.

Joey never showed up at his company's annual parties each year. But at the end of the day he'd claim he was there, and narrate everything that happened at the party. No one saw him.

The rumor of Joey's disappearance spreads quickly at his workplace, and those that worked with him are horrified by the news. Some try to cope with the news while others run around the office yelling like crazy people. Joey's disappearance is considered as one of the biggest mysteries ever.

Despite all odds, Joey was a dedicated engineer. He knew his job well; everyone loved Joey at his workplace, including the president.

They all praised him for his invention.

"We lost one of our best workers, and he will be missed," they laments.

Meanwhile Pastor Wright wants to celebrate Joey's departure back to heaven. She fires a pistol into the air.

"We are celebrating. Tasha and Joan, it's time for you to move on," she says. Pastor Wright turns around and looks at everyone.

"Please, if you know anyone looking for a roommate, tell them to investigate the person first. You never know, they might end up with a ghost or another terrible person."

"Please stop that," Tasha scolds Pastor Wright. "You are hurting my feelings. You don't know my husband. He was the best man I have ever known."

The pastor looks at her in an unusual way.

"I must leave now," Tasha says, and grabs her bag. "Joan, I wish you the best."

They hug each other and say their goodbyes.

"Goodbye, Tasha. Take care of the kids. If you ever need my help don't hesitate to call me."

Pastor Wright is aggravated at Joan's kindness to Tasha. "Joan, I didn't know you were that generous."

Joan shrugs.

Tasha heads towards the door. Joan's friends think it's time to leave as well, so they follow Tasha to the front door. As the door opens, reporters flood in with questions for Joan.

"Joan, where is your husband? How can an accomplished engineer like Joey Noel simply disappear inside the house?" the reporters were very aggressive.

"How do you respond to the rumor that you were married to a ghost? Could you share some of your experiences with him?"

"What was he like as a husband?" another reporter asks. "The inquiry minds wants to know—what's special about him?"

Pastor Wright pushes the reporters back, and fires a few round into the air to scare the reporters. "Don't worry, Joan. I'll answer their questions. Trust me," Pastor Wright promises her, and fire more rounds into the air.

Two months after Joey's disappearance, Joan starts having morning sickness. She panics, and fears the worse that she might be pregnant with the child of a ghost.

Author's Experiences with Ghosts.

I have experienced the presence of ghost twice in my life time. The first one was at the age of twelve in a rural village. I was going to the market with my grandmother who was 65 at the time. My grandmother and I were walking on a sidewalk on a major road when I looked to my left; I saw a pretty well dressed lady—approximately in her late thirties carrying a fancy basket filled with groceries, with her feet floating on the air. She was coming back from the market. Instead of going straight down the road, she headed towards an isolated narrow pathway leading to a forest. When she saw me, she quickly looked away. I tapped my grandmother on her back. "Did you see that lady?" I asked. "Her feet are not touching the ground. She's going to the forest with her groceries. No one lives there, Grandma. It's a farming area." My grandmother looked towards the forest, but saw no one.

"I can't see her," my grandmother replied.

The woman turned around and looked at us and continued going her way. Then my mother looked at me, and said, "She's the departed—she lives beyond. They come to the market to buy and sell like normal people. She's going back home."

The second experience was in 2007 in an apartment complex in Tempe, Arizona. I was leaning on the rail close to the stairs with my friend, Wilson. And we saw a man in short and T-Shirt on the stairway coming towards us—his feet seemed like it was floating in the air. About a step before he could reach us, he disappeared. "What happened to the guy that was coming towards us?" Wilson asked.

"He just disappeared right there," I told Wilson. We went to every corner looking for him, but he was gone. Then it hit us, we had seen a ghost.

This is a work of fiction. Names, characters, places and incidents either are the product of the author's imagination or are used fictitiously. Any resemblance to actual person living or dead, events or locals is entirely coincidence.

All rights reserved.
Published in United States by Santrac Production.

No parts of this publication may be reproduced in whole or in parts, or stored in retrieval system, or transmitted in any form or by any means, electronically, photocopying, recording, or otherwise, without written permission of the publisher. For information regarding the permission, write to Santrac Producton, P O Box 8698 Phoenix, Arizona 85066

www.ingramcontent.com/pod-product-compliance
Lightning Source LLC
Chambersburg PA
CBHW020247150626
46552CB00020B/615